MERCY KILLING

THE HAUNTING OF GHOUL HOUSE

NEIL SATER

WEST KILBRIDE LLC

Cover Design by James, GoOnWrite.com

Front Cover Image Created By Chris Esch

Library of Congress Control Number: 2024910556

ISBN: 979-8-9885508-2-2

Published by: West Kilbride LLC 6618 Morningside Dr. Cleveland OH 44141

First edition - 2024

Sign up for Neil Sater's newsletter through his website:

https://authorsater.com/

For my father, Bernie Sater, who passed away while I was working on this book. He was a wonderful man and an incredible dad. Kind and strong, smart and humble, and the most unflappable person I've ever known.

CONTENTS

Chapter 1

Witch Hunt

July 15, 1936

W HEN THE BOYS HEARD the thunderous crash, they shot one another stunned glances. Without a word, they frantically reeled in their fishing lines, flung the poles onto the grassy bank, and sprinted along the pond's edge toward the sound.

"Wait for me!" Hank shouted after Jimmy, who outpaced him as usual.

"Hurry up, slowpoke!" Jimmy yelled over his shoulder, not slowing down for his younger brother. Hank was barely eight, but Jimmy was well past ten, so he always held the upper hand in competitions. "She ain't gonna just sit there and wait for us!"

Tangled tree roots furrowed the trail when they entered the woods, slowing their pace. They bounded along the creek-side path that meandered, sloping downward, toward the abandoned house. Holding up where the woods opened into a clearing behind the decaying structure, Jimmy crouched just inside the edge of the brush.

Hank jogged up beside him. "She there?" He gasped the question between pants, while leaning on his knees.

"Shhh!" Jimmy shook his head in that irritated-older-brother way.

The huddled boys gazed at the forsaken Gould farmhouse. Pop reckoned one of the earliest white settlers in Ohio had built the simple house over a century ago. Now gray and rickety, its age was the least of its woes. The home had fallen into disrepair, with windows broken, rotten clapboards dangling, weeds and overgrowth steadily consuming it.

Shirley Gould, an elderly widow, had lived and died there. A couple of years before Jimmy was born, Pop had found her body on the kitchen floor a few weeks after she had toppled off a stepladder. Shirley's overflowing mailbox triggered Pop's realization that he hadn't seen her in a while. When he pulled his 1922 Ford Model TT truck up to the house, he caught a whiff of the heatwave-enhanced stench.

It did not take long before stories turned into Homer County legends. It was said Shirley could be heard wailing at night from inside the dilapidated home. By the time Hank was a schoolboy, kids in the schoolhouse shared elaborate tales about Shirley going mad and murdering her husband, Harold. The way it went, Harold's ghost had killed Shirley in revenge, and now *both* spirits haunted the house.

Pop had laughed heartily when the boys told him what the kids were saying. "Shirley didn't kill Harold! He died in the hospital, the first year of the Spanish flu."

Hank had to admit Pop knew better than the kids did, and anyway, he'd never heard wails coming from the abandoned home. But this didn't prompt him to dispute the folklore. He wore an odd badge of honor, living so close to the legendary site, and the brothers' own intrigue toward the haunted house grew steadily with time.

Out of school for the summer, the boys had been hearing a booming crash on the metal roof of the Gould farmhouse a couple of times each day.

"I'll bet it's a witch," Jimmy had said.

And that was pretty much all it took to decide it was Shirley Gould, now a witch, landing on the rusty tin roof upon returning from her broomstick rides. It was a tantalizing explanation for imaginative boys with little else to occupy their minds. The summer days were long and lazy since neither of them was old enough yet to be handed serious duties on the farm. So, having time on their hands, they grew more determined with each passing day to catch a glimpse of the dreaded hag.

Now they had their chance.

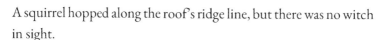

A squirrel hopped along the roof's ridge line, but there was no witch in sight.

"Maybe she went inside already," Hank said.

Jimmy only shrugged and continued scanning the scene.

Hank was glad for the opportunity to catch his breath at a safe distance.

"We're going in." Without waiting for a response, Jimmy stood and began walking down the path toward the house.

Tagging along hesitantly, Hank kept a few steps behind. They gave the dwelling sideways glances as they passed it on their way to the front. After wading through the tangle that had once been the front yard, they held up at the open doorway. Hank sidled close to Jimmy, and together, they peered into the uninviting murk. The interior smelled of mildew and rot.

"C'mon," Jimmy whispered, tiptoeing onto the canted sandstone doorstep.

Hank's shoulders slumped. He almost protested, suggesting they go get Pop to take them in, but swallowed the thought. He told himself at least Jimmy wasn't scouting the pitch-dark cellar; there was no telling what might be lurking down *there*. Hank tried not to think about that. With his heart beating in his ears, he reluctantly drew forward.

When Jimmy stepped over the threshold, the floor creaked, followed by a screech from upstairs. Hank ducked under the door frame as a large bird fluttered away in a cacophony of squawks and a frenzy of wing flaps. He turned and looked to the sky, but whatever it was must have flown off in the opposite direction.

Hank straggled inside, staying within arm's reach of Jimmy. As they moved into the center of the main room, the sagging floor joists groaned. A mouse scurried into the adjoining room, followed by another, then one more.

Having explored this level of the building countless times, the boys were familiar with its contents. They had picked through the row of wooden milk crates lining the main interior wall many times, leaving behind a random collection of worthless odds and ends: ancient, yellowed newspapers, empty canning jars, molding leather shoes, rusting parts of tools. A wooden table with broken legs tilted crazily in the corner, too ravaged for any scavenger to bother snagging.

They snaked their way through the debris strewn about the floor and peeked into the back room, the kitchen. With no sign of Witch Shirley, Jimmy, mischief in his eyes, bee-lined for the newspaper crate and fished out the 1920 Sears Catalog he'd buried in the bottom.

Hank let out an air groan.

Even in the gloom, Jimmy didn't need a book marker to find pages 136-137. "Ooh, la, la," he whispered, wagging his eyebrows at Hank. Ma called him "Mr. Tom Foolery" when he acted like this, whatever that meant.

"C'mon, Jimmy," Hank pleaded quietly. It was not like he hadn't also found a strange allure in the women's undergarments images, but this wasn't the time.

Jimmy took one last good look, like capturing a portrait on a canvas inside his ten-year-old mind. He blew a kiss at the page, then closed the catalog and tucked it back into its hiding place. Without further delay, he rose and headed straight for the stairway.

"Jimmy—" Hank called after him.

Suddenly, a scuffle commenced upstairs, then faded into silence.

The boys froze. Jimmy gave Hank a backward glance, and their mouths fell ajar in unison. Jimmy soon broke eye contact and resumed moving toward the foot of the stairs, gesturing for Hank to follow. Instead, Hank started turning toward the exit hole, then stiffened, shifting his eyes over to Jimmy as he strode forward.

They had only ventured into the upper level once before, and even then, they had gone just far enough for their heads to clear the floor. After little more than a swift glance, they had lost their nerve and scrambled away. And that was *before* they had started hearing the witch landing on the roof.

Jimmy turned and shot a big-brother glare, silently threatening to brand the word "CHICKEN" across Hank's forehead. He impatiently waved Hank his way. With a dry swallow, Hank obeyed.

Shoulder to shoulder, the boys angled into the narrow passageway and gaped upward. The steep stairs resembled a ladder more so than steps. A quick getaway via this treacherous route would be impossible.

Jimmy led the way up the perilous ladder-steps, and Hank shadowed him with his teeth clenched so tightly his jaw was aching by the halfway point.

The scuffling, which sounded like a rake being dragged over the wooden floor planks, resumed the moment they reached the top, and the room, which appeared empty, suddenly filled with the echoes of a chilling hiss. Both boys recoiled in wide-eyed terror. Hank leaned back against the wall and shuddered, trying not to tumble down the stairway. Shreds of moldy wallpaper hung from the surface, grasping at him like bony fingers. Before he could flee, Jimmy reached over and grabbed Hank by the shirt, holding him in place.

Raising his free hand, Jimmy pointed across the room.

Hank nodded. Following the roof pitch, the sloping ceiling ended in what Pop called a "knee wall," just like the short wall at the back end of the boy's bedroom. Jimmy's finger vectored toward a half-open closet door built into the far end of the knee wall. The unhuman noise erupted from this tiny crawlspace.

In his child-mind's eye, Hank pictured Shirley crouching in the shadows of the nook, her witch face contorted in anger at the intrusion. She hissed in a threatening, guttural tone that grew in volume, then paused while she drew a breath before restarting a new crescendo.

When she hissed once again, louder yet, Hank covered his ears with his hands and squeezed. Jimmy let go of Hank's shirt and spun around, as if even he, too, had lost his courage. The panicked brothers scrabbled down the tight staircase, practically tumbling over each other as they went. Each leaped down the final remaining steps, then out the front door like fleeing cats, with Jimmy passing Hank as they sprinted across the overgrown yard toward the sanctuary of their home.

After supper, the boys cajoled Pop into going back with them to the old house.

He walked in first, gingerly testing the floor as he headed for the stairway. "Won't be long before this place will be too far gone to enter."

In response to his voice, the scratching and hissing noises resumed. Undaunted, Pop mounted the steps. With his dad showing no outward sign of anxiety, Hank felt his own fear tempered. He fell in behind Pop, and this time, Jimmy brought up the rear. The volume of the hideous sounds grew as the trio ascended, but Pop kept a steady gait.

The boys held back at the top of the stairwell, anxiously watching Pop while he crossed the room. He made his way toward the closet, still testing the floor with each stride. The hiss bloomed into a roar as he neared the opening, drowning out his footfalls.

"Pop, no!" Hank cried.

His dad turned and put the "shhh" finger against his lips.

Hank looked at Jimmy, who stared at Pop with saucer eyes.

Pop set the oil lamp he'd brought on the floor. After fishing a box of matches out from the bib pocket of his overalls, he struck one into a flame and adjusted the wick with one hand while lighting it with the other. From the shadowy corner of the room, his face began glowing under the flickering light.

The setting fell deathly quiet as Pop reached for the small door, but when he tugged on it, the hinges creaked, shattering the silence.

Hank's breathing stalled while his heart fluttered like a hummingbird.

Pop squatted, gathered the lamp, and lifted it into the miniature door frame. Squinting, he stared into the gloom for a spell. "Come see, boys."

The boys gave each other a wary glance before inching across the room, their pace almost stalling as they drew in.

Pop motioned them onward.

With Jimmy close by, Hank tilted forward in a crouch, readying himself to jump aside if the witch came bursting forth. He cautiously peered into the crawlspace, waiting for his eyes to adjust to the dim light. To his shock, there was no witch. Instead, two white fluffy balls were cowering in the closet's back corner.

"Baby turkey vultures," Pop announced, letting out a belly laugh. "They're nesting here. I reckon that's the parents you hear coming home to feed them. Adults are giant birds, so they'd make a real racket landing on the loose tin roof."

"But..." Jimmy trailed off and said nothing else.

Hank studied the creatures with a crinkled nose, feeling his cheeks turning hot. Although they had already grown to the size of a milk bottle, the birds, covered in white, fuzzy baby feathers, looked cuddly and harmless. Despite their cute appearance, their beady eyes stared back with hostility at the unwelcome visitors. One of them hissed, and the other immediately joined in.

Pop chortled. "These critters are called buzzards. They make those sounds to scare off intruders. We best leave them alone before their ma or pa returns." After pushing the door back into the position it had been in, he switched off the oil lamp and started for the stairwell.

When Hank turned to his brother, Jimmy was frozen in position, his mouth hanging open. With a confusing mix of emotions swirling in his own head, Hank pushed himself upright, which seemed to break Jimmy free from his stupor.

Jimmy reached out and manacled his fingers around Hank's wrist. "This don't mean the house ain't haunted," he said under his breath.

Hank shook his head. "Nope. It don't."

"I bet the buzzard parents are coming and going through here," Pop said from the other end of the room, near the top of the ladder-steps. He leaned out the aperture that had once been a window, craning his neck to examine the eaves above.

Hank and Jimmy trudged over. Stepping up to the window hole, the boys flanked Pop on opposite sides.

When Hank looked out at the scrubby stretch of property that had once been the home's yard, an out-of-place black scar in the rear corner immediately caught his attention. A long, narrow opening marred the ground of the tiny Gould family cemetery. "What's that, Pop?"

Pop tilted his head down and followed the line of Hank's pointing finger. He raised a hand to scratch his head and asked, "What in Sam Hill?"

All three of them stared at the scene, trying to make sense of it. After a long moment of silence, Pop asked what they all wanted to know. "What the devil happened there?"

A fresh mound of dirt sat beside Shirley Gould's open grave.

CHAPTER 2

―◆◇◆―

ZOMBIE HUNT

HALLOWEEN, 1970

B RENDA MITCHELL FELT A gush of relief when the movie credits began rolling. Now that it was safe, she released her death clutch on Kathy's arm and sat upright. They rose with the rest of the throng, and as they waited to merge into the aisle, Kathy turned to her with wide eyes and a big grin. "That was way out, man!"

Brenda nodded to her best friend. But while Kathy seemed to have been energized by the movie, Brenda felt exhausted and numb, never having seen a flick like *that* before.

In the smoking section at the back of the theater, a long-haired, senior-class hunk Brenda recognized from high school clomped toward his flower-child girlfriend with outstretched arms. She giggled and squealed as he reached for her shoulders. Feigning fright, she fell into his grasp. When they started necking, Brenda averted her gaze.

Orange and black crepe paper adorned the double-door exit-way, sprucing up the theater for the Halloween matinee. After they passed into the lobby, Kathy peeled out of the horde and stopped to examine the film's poster, as if, having just experienced it, she might find new meaning in the montage of terrorized faces and

undead beings. Mutant green capitalized words stood out against
the black-and-white images:

NIGHT OF THE LIVING DEAD
THEY WON'T STAY DEAD

After a hasty glance, Brenda turned instead to the flyer mounted
beside the movie poster and stared at the face of the smiling boy in
the center.

<u>MISSING</u>
Dennis Harmon – 10 years old

The flyers had been plastered all over Homer County for over a
year, but the boy remained missing. With a shudder, Brenda pulled
away. Eager to get out, back into what was left of the daylight, she
tugged on Kathy's arm.

Folding back into the streaming crowd, Kathy said, "Yeah, let's go
look for the *real* zombie now."

"Did you notice they never called them zombies in the movie?"
Brenda asked as they approached the Clarkton Theater exit.

"Ghouls." Kathy pendulum'd her head from side to side while she
considered this. "Same thing." She arched her eyebrows. "Time for
a ghoul-hunt."

When they stepped into the fading late afternoon sun, Brenda
asked, "Are you sure? After that hairy movie?"

"You're not chicken, are you?"

Brenda scoffed. "It's just a stupid legend."

Kathy skipped around the front of her father's pickup truck on her way to the driver's side. "It's Halloween night. What else are we going to do? Go trick-or-treating?"

Now that they were sixteen years old and driving, everything had changed. But Brenda made her half-hearted case when she pulled open her door and leaned into the cab. "I like candy."

Kathy laughed as she climbed behind the wheel. "We're not kids anymore."

The sun slipped behind the horizon as the Chevy pickup truck left Clarkton's commercial zone behind. With dusk spreading through the autumn countryside, Kathy yanked out the headlight knob.

When a piano began playing on the radio, Brenda sprang for the volume dial, cranking it clockwise, then backing off until the worn-out speaker stopped crackling. She immersed herself in the hit tune, which felt like a perfect salve on her raw nerves, still pulsing from Romero's unsettling yet spellbinding film. Soon, she began singing along with Simon & Garfunkel about a bridge over troubled water.

Kathy sang too, although with nowhere near Brenda's level of gusto. A big fan of The Who, Kathy's fandom had mushroomed to an obsession level since they released *Tommy*.

As she belted out the chorus, Brenda glimpsed Kassell's Hill, the tallest point in the region, silhouetted in the distance. They were more than halfway there.

The last of the remaining daylight was leaching from the western sky when they turned off the winding two-lane state highway onto Township Road 223. Kathy tapped the foot switch to toggle on the high beams, illuminating the latticework of mostly bare tree branches canopying the country road. They snaked along the winding gravel route through the Salem Valley, heading for Shirley Gould's abandoned farmhouse.

Brenda had been too embarrassed to admit she lived near the Gould house when she was younger. There was so much gossip about it being haunted that she had been afraid the other kids would tag her as weird by association. When she reached high school, most of her classmates decided the place was cool—particularly in the past two years, after *Night of the Living Dead* came out. Since the movie's release, the kids gave the Gould house a new nickname: "Ghoul House."

"There's a pullout on the right side of the road, just before we go down the hill," Brenda said. "We need to park there and walk, so my parents won't see us."

"Isn't Hank busy with harvest?" Kathy asked with a giggle. They thought it funny to refer to each other's parents by their first names, though not in their presence, of course.

Brenda nodded. "But if he found out I was going near that house, he'd come unglued." She pointed at the turnout. "Right there."

Kathy steered over, brushing against the weeds along the side of the roadway as she tucked in, then pushed in the light knob before cutting the engine.

As Brenda slid out the passenger side, Kathy leaned over and popped open the glove compartment. She removed the flashlight on the top, then rooted under the other junk before pulling out a revolver.

Brenda's mouth fell open. "Where did *that* come from?"

"It's my dad's. He keeps it in here."

"We never talked about a *gun* being part of the dare."

"You saw the movie: 'Kill the brain, and you kill the ghoul.'"

"It's a *movie*."

Kathy closed the glove box door and held the firearm under the dome light, verifying it was loaded. "Right, but everybody says Shirley Gould is a zombie, so this is our protection. We're lucky my dad keeps it in here."

Brenda rolled her eyes. There was no way she would be able to convince Kathy to leave the gun behind. When Kathy got something lodged in her head, there was no prying it out. Like this stupid too-close-to-home odyssey, for instance, which Kathy had insisted on as their Halloween entertainment, despite the risk of being caught by Brenda's parents.

It was true that everyone talked about Shirley Gould's home being haunted, and most recently, how Shirley had crawled out of the grave to roam the countryside as a flesh-eating zombie. Although Brenda had never actually seen anything inexplicable there, she had been as afraid of and fascinated by Ghoul House as anyone. Even her dad admitted Shirley's grave had been dug up back when he was a boy, and no, her body had never been found. So, technically, Shirley *could* be a zombie.

They won't stay dead.

Brenda shook the movie's tagline away and hurried to catch up to Kathy, who had set off down the slope.

"I'm keeping the flashlight off until we get to the house," Kathy said, sort of implying she was making a token concession for bringing the gun.

Brenda gave the okay sign and whispered, "Good plan."

Aside from the rhythmic crunching of gravel underfoot, they remained silent during their quarter-mile trek. A light fog had settled in the valley, clouding the rising crescent moon like a cataract over an eye. When the girls rounded the country road's bend, the Gould homestead emerged, squatting before them, half-smothered in overgrowth. They halted to take in the sight. Brenda noted how its moldering gray siding shone eerily in the twilight.

Almost like it's glowing.

She said nothing, though, and when Kathy made no mention of it, Brenda assured herself, *It's just a trick of light.*

A sharp breeze blew, tearing a squall of autumn leaves from the surrounding trees. Brenda looked up, spotting the first stars glimmering in the cloudless sky between twitching skeleton-finger tree branches. She wrapped her arms around each other and pressed them against her torso. Although it had been a warm day, the air had turned chilly as night had fallen.

"Shirrr-leeey!" Kathy called without warning, holding the gun forward with one hand, the unlit flashlight clasped in the other. She leaped across the ditch, stopping at the crest of the embankment to watch and listen. "Are you home?"

"Shut up!" Brenda admonished from behind her. "My mom might hear!"

"Pfft. Eliza can't hear us from here, man," Kathy said over her shoulder. She moved toward the house, picking her way through the scrub.

Brenda crossed the ditch and followed her friend's path through the overgrowth. As her bell-bottom cuffs caught on the sticks and dying vegetation, her eyes swept between the Gould family burial plot behind the house on one side, and the lights of her own home in the distance on the other.

Her mother would be cooking dinner. Out of sight in the field behind the barn, the combine grumbled, her father harvesting the corn crop, guided by an array of lights. It would be a long day for him, but with rain in the forecast for tomorrow, he would keep at it until the job was done. As Hank Mitchell was always quick to point out, harvest was dictated by weather and the season, and when the conditions were right, farmers better not put it off. Or, as non-farmers often say, "Make hay while the sun shines."

The front door of the Gould homestead was long gone, leaving a gaping portal into darkness. Kathy brushed her way through the weeds, heading toward the coal-black maw of the ruins. Slowing as she drew in, she called once again, "Shirrr-leeey?" She chuckled nervously this time. When she mounted the sandstone step, she turned on the flashlight and pointed it inside the dwelling.

Brenda sidled up beside her friend but remained a half step behind. When she caught a whiff of the musty smell of mold and decay wafting out from the gloomy interior, she bristled and covered her nose.

The light beam sliced through the murk, illuminating remnants of scattered junk. A mouse scurried across the floor, disappearing into a pile of empty tin cans. Kathy leaned into the opening, revolver at the ready. "Any flesh-eating ghouls in Ghoul House?" Without waiting for a reply, she stepped onto the threshold.

Brenda gasped. "Don't go in there!"

Since she was a little girl, her father had warned her, "Don't ever go into that house. It ain't safe to enter." She never had.

Kathy did not respond. She swept the light across the floor, pausing to examine a collection of canning jars with various amalgams trapped under rusting lids. "Ew, it's grody in here." She took a step forward.

"Kathy, please...my dad says it's not safe."

Kathy blew a raspberry and shook her head at the ridiculous notion. "Don't sweat it."

From the stoop, Brenda glanced in the direction of her home.

Kathy kicked debris aside as she moved, clearing a path as she headed for the stairway. She pointed the beam up the stairs. "Shirley?" She turned back and shone the light on Brenda. "Are you coming?"

Brenda shielded her face from the glare. "No way." Feeling Kathy's eyes on her, she pursed her lips and tried not to blink.

With a dramatic huff, Kathy turned back around and took another step toward the stairway. The floor made a loud cracking sound under her weight. She froze. A sustained groan followed, then diminished. Kathy held her statue pose for a spell before pivoting her head one way, then the other, slowly, like trying to regain trust in the ruins she had ventured into.

She gave a little shrug and took another pace. Without warning, the rotted joist gave way, and she plummeted through a hole that opened in the floor, the way those trap doors work in the cartoons. She yelped as she dropped. A muffled thud followed, and a split second later, the gun fired, the sound dampened between the cellar's dirt floor and the decaying wood above. With Kathy's flashlight gone, the interior went totally dark.

Brenda gasped into her palm. She waited for a terror-stricken moment. "Kathy?" Her shaking voice sounded weak.

No response.

Brenda nudged as far forward as she could without crossing the threshold, leaned in, cupped her hands around her mouth, and shouted, "Kathy!"

"Shit!"

Brenda felt a rush of relief at hearing her friend's muted voice, the sound absorbed by the moldy surfaces of her surroundings. "Are you okay?"

Kathy took a while to respond, as though she was trying to assess that for herself. "I'm not sure. The flashlight's broken. I accidentally pulled the trigger."

Panic arose in Brenda as she imagined what it would be like being plunged into the creepy hellhole, now stuck, blind in the inky cellar, completely alone. She pressed a hand against her pounding chest. "Can you move?"

Again, Kathy did not immediately answer. "I think so...but it's pitch black down here!"

"The ceiling's low. You'd better crawl."

Kathy groaned. "Crawl where?"

"The cellar opening. It's at the back of the house." Although Brenda knew it would not be far, she also knew that down there in the abyss, it might as well be at the other end of the cornfield.

"I can't...go crawling through the dark!" Kathy fell silent for a moment as if she was scrabbling for some other option, and Brenda could sense her friend's dread blossoming as the seconds ticked by. "You've got to get me out of here!"

Brenda turned and looked at her house. Staring at the lit kitchen window, she yelled over her shoulder, "I'll go get my mom!"

"Hurry!"

Hindered by darkness and the overgrowth, Brenda crossed through the yard as rapidly as she could manage. When she reached the gravel roadway, she quickened her pace, bolting toward her home with a wary eye on the lights moving across the field behind the barn.

When she burst in the back door, her mother, peeling potatoes at the kitchen counter, jumped. Eliza Mitchell gave a questioning look as she held her hand against her chest and drew in a deep breath.

"Mom, you're going to be mad..." Brenda panted half a dozen times, giving her warning a chance to sink in, hoping it might dull her mom's response to what she would say next. "Kathy fell into the cellar at the Gould house. We need to get her out."

This time Brenda did not pause, figuring a flurry of activity might stave off questions. She stepped beside her mother and flung open the junk drawer, rifling through it until she came across the flashlight. She switched it on and shone the light at the table. "Do we have another?"

The tactic seemed to work. Her mother opened her mouth, then closed it, dropped the potato peeler, wiped her hands on the towel, and went about tussling with her apron ties. "Your father keeps one in the barn, but I don't know where."

"This will have to do, then." Brenda Mitchell pushed open the screen door and waved for her mother to follow.

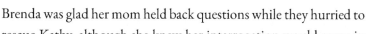

Brenda was glad her mom held back questions while they hurried to rescue Kathy, although she knew her interrogation would come in time.

The combine rumbled through the field, its cone of light creeping across the slope. Although she was pretty sure they were out of her dad's eyeshot, Brenda avoided turning on the flashlight until they were crossing the front yard of the Gould house, lest he catch a glimpse of a beam bouncing where one did not belong. Fortunately, the light fog had cleared, so the moon cast enough light they could see the ground.

Slowing her pace, Brenda toggled on the flashlight. Just as she pointed it into the front entrance, Kathy gave out a muffled scream, and the gun went off.

Brenda flinched and froze. Her mother grasped her shoulders from behind, pulling her against her body.

"Was that a gun?" Eliza panted the question into Brenda's ear.

Brenda nodded.

"I don't know what's happening, but maybe we need your father."

"Not yet." Brenda could not prevent her mother from telling her dad about this, but if they got out of the situation without his involvement, there was at least a chance the whole thing could be kept a secret from him.

Brenda pulled away from her mom, sweeping the beam across the derelict structure as she approached. "Kathy?"

Kathy screamed, and the gun fired again.

Brenda and her mother both halted in their tracks.

"There's something down here!"

Brenda's mind seized with a jolt of terror. *Something's down there? Something* what? She ordered herself to remain calm. Kathy, who would understandably be freaking out by now, would *need* her to stay calm.

Steering the light into the front door hole, she followed the beam. A hand wrapped around her waist as she drew in on the entrance stoop. She recoiled and turned, only to discover it was just her mom.

When she panned across the room with the flashlight, she saw only the shifting mosaic of shadows cast by the debris strewn about the floor. She trained the beam on the ragged aperture through which the sound of Kathy's sobbing emanated.

"Hang on...we're coming!" Brenda yelled.

"Hurry! There's a zombie down here!"

Brenda's heart stopped as she tried to come to grips with Kathy's claim. Could this just be a Halloween prank? Except, if Kathy was messing around, she sure was doing a damn good job of it.

Brenda reached for her mother's hand and then pulled her away from the entrance hole. She led the way along the front of the house, wondering when she had last held her mom's hand. It felt particularly strange to be acting as the guide.

Thorns snagged on Brenda's jean jacket sleeve as she pressed through the thickening tangles. She shortened her strides as she approached the east end of the dwelling, then peered around the corner to confirm they were alone. Proceeding down that side, she waded into a heap of fallen leaves. Her mother held her hand tight and followed, and together, they swooshed through the drift toward the rear of the structure, while Brenda nervously eyed the silhouettes of the Gould family plot in the corner of the yard.

With her heart thudding into her ears, Brenda pitched around the back corner of the building and shined the flashlight ahead with a trembling hand. About fifteen feet away, the ancient sandstone cellar steps, bookended by crumbling dry-stacked stone walls, led down into the earth under the house.

Brenda hesitated, sweeping her surroundings with the beam of light. The crudely carved sandstone blocks framing the entrance tilted precariously inward as if a good solid kick might cave the wall in, bringing the entire thing cascading down upon itself and into the cellar.

Kathy cried out from the interior side of the foundation, "Where are you?"

"Almost there!" Brenda trotted to the stairway, pulling her mom along.

At the top of the stairs, she froze, pointing the light down the steep steps of the passageway. How many times had she peered down into that impenetrable darkness? She had dared herself to venture into the cellar countless times in the past, but never managed to pass beyond the black hole opening at the foot of the stairway. Could she do it now?

Kathy whimpered from somewhere inside the cellar. "Please..."

Brenda braced herself, leaned forward, and steered the light into the void, focusing past the massive spider web stretched across the upper part of the opening like a taped-off murder scene. Straining for a glimpse of her friend, the light revealed only the rubble of a few stray foundation rocks and wooden structural pieces that had fallen to the dirt floor.

A surge of nausea overcame her, leaving her feeling like she had just climbed off the Witch's Twirl ride at the Homer County Fair. She swallowed hard, fighting the urge to throw up.

Eliza released Brenda's hand, grabbed the flashlight, and then rushed down the steps. "I'm coming!"

An unnatural stillness permeating the cellar stifled the sound of her mother's voice, muting it without echo. Eliza swept away the spider web, crouched, and scrambled inside, her guiding light vanishing from Brenda's field of view.

Alone in the darkness, Brenda felt a chill slither down her spine. With her jaw clenched, she looked over both shoulders to survey the surrounding nightscape, then took a tentative step down, then another. A dank, pungent odor thickened while the air stagnated with her descent.

Halfway down, she squatted and peered into the depths of the cellar, the sweeping flashlight beam illuminating the space in jumbled flashes, stirring shadows into life. On the opposite end, the collapsed section of the floor dangled from above. Her mom, bent over because the ceiling was no taller than herself, chased after the light in that direction. Suddenly, just beyond the hanging wreckage, the beam fell on Kathy. Cowering from a seated fetal position, she held the revolver in one hand while shielding her eyes from the glare of the flashlight with the other.

The gun was pointed at a mass on the dirt floor, within arm's reach of Kathy. What *was* that? Brenda squinted. Dull, charcoal-black eye sockets stared out from a shriveled head. Jagged teeth, bared by receding lips, shimmered in the light.

Brenda resisted the urge to back away and forced herself to lean closer for a better view. Was it...a pig? *A dead pig.* It looked...*mummified!*

The shock of the sight disrupted Brenda's balance, sending her tipping forward and falling into the entranceway. She shot out her hands, catching hold of the moss-fuzzed stone wall just in time. With a push, she righted herself and returned to a crouch. She went back to examining the scene.

Since domestic swine sometimes escape from their farm and stray off into the countryside, Brenda was not exactly surprised to spot one down there. There was no telling how long ago this pig had perished, though. How much time would it take for its carcass to desiccate like that in the cellar's cool, dark, and dry environment? God knows. Heck, it might have been there for decades.

Eliza kneeled beside Kathy, still sobbing, her revolver trained on the gruesome remains. After wrapping one arm around Kathy, Eliza pulled the teenager close. She placed the flashlight on the dirt floor, and with her free hand, gently removed the firearm from Kathy's grasp.

"It's just a pig, honey," Eliza said.

Kathy stared at the withered swine, spotlighted by the flashlight beam. "I bumped into it..." She shivered with the thought, then inhaled a long, quivering breath. "I thought...it was...a zombie."

"It's only a pig," Eliza repeated.

Brenda felt relieved by her mother's reassuring words. If the tension of the past fifteen minutes hadn't been so slow to leave her, she might have been inclined to laugh at the situation.

Eliza pulled Kathy to her feet and began brushing her off.

Kathy seemed unable to move. She simply stared at the mummified pig.

"You get the light," Eliza told her.

Kathy broke free from her daze. She nodded slowly, then picked up the flashlight and pointed it at the carcass, trying to absorb the fact it was not a ghoul she'd felt in the darkness, after all.

With her arm around Kathy's waist, Eliza pulled her toward the stairway. "You girls have a lot of explaining to do," she said to Brenda with raised eyebrows.

Brenda nodded solemnly.

"But just to me. It's best if your father doesn't hear about this."

A wave of relief washed over Brenda. If her mom kept this a secret, her dad would never find out she had broken her promise to stay out of the old house. Brenda certainly wasn't ever going to tell him.

CHAPTER 3

POSSESSION

JUNE 25, 2002

O N SUCH A PERFECT summer day, Hank Mitchell could never have imagined the descent into horror his life was about to take.

Throughout his 74 years, fishing had always been his favorite diversion. On this beautiful evening, the fish were lively while the mosquitos slacked off. When the sun dropped toward the horizon, stretching crimson trails across the sky above his Homer County farm, Hank told himself, *Better head back, Old Man.* Proud of how well he had held up through the years, the nickname he had given himself reflected his verifiable age rather than his physical or cognitive state. He gathered his fishing gear and rifle.

With his .22 at the ready, he tiptoed across the dam, scanning the embankment for any sign of groundhogs denning in the earthworks. Unlike most farmers, Hank mostly tolerated the undeniably cute creatures. Except this spot was off-limits. If groundhogs tunneled into the dam, they would weaken it, which could bring catastrophic results. Fortunately, he saw no sign of such menace.

He followed the lane bisecting a field of corn his tenant farmer had cultivated, admiring it as he passed. *Knee-high by the fourth of July* was the old saying. This stand reached above his waist, and in some patches, approached shoulder height—and Independence Day was still over a week off. A scarecrow had been erected near the mid-point of the lane, donning overalls and a flannel shirt stuffed with straw, topped with a burlap sack head. "Evening, sir," Hank said as he passed.

The scarecrow merely glowered down the pathway with unblinking black button eyes.

Movement caught Hank's attention when he reached the point where the field ended and the trail opened into the clearing behind his barn. His heart leaped at the sight of his wife crossing the back lawn, heading from the house toward the barn. It was not so much *where* Eliza was walking—although even this was odd since she seldom went to the barn—it was *how* she moved.

Eliza lurched. She shambled, like Boris Karloff, in that old Frankenstein movie.

What in Sam Hill? Hank's mind scrambled, trying to make sense of the scene. Eliza had recently complained of headaches and double-vision, but there had been nothing strange like this.

"Eliza?" Hank called from behind the barn.

She stopped and glared. Hank noticed something in her hand for the first time: a knitting needle, which she pointed at him as if it were a miniature sword. She had been knitting in the parlor when Hank left the house. Her hand wavered, and after a moment she broke her stare, turning back toward the barn door, which he had left open.

Hank dropped his fishing gear and rifle, hastening toward her. He rounded the front corner of the barn just before she disappeared into the darkness. "Eliza?"

She halted and looked his way, studying him with a rabid look, aiming the knitting needle in his direction. He raised his hands in surrender like television criminals sometimes do when the police have them cornered. A surge of fear took root in Hank's brain. *The devil got into her.* As silly as this idea sounded, it was the only explanation he could muster.

Eliza turned toward the barn. When Hank took two long steps forward, she hurried away in an off-kilter gait, plowing into the sawhorse just inside the darkened interior. She let out a tortured whimper like a wounded dog and crumpled to the hard-packed dirt floor, losing her grip on the knitting needle.

Hank ran to her, taking an angle that kept him between her and the needle. "Oh, Eliza! You alright, dear?" He crouched, reaching for her with both hands.

She cowered and rolled away, but soon bumped against a tractor tire barrier. From the dirt floor, she turned, and the look on her face said she knew she could not escape. With a panicked shake of her head, Eliza blurted, "Who *are* you?"

Stunned by the question, he froze, feeling as though a pitchfork had been plunged into his chest. Backing away, he pulled the John Deere cap off his head and dropped it on the ground. He immediately felt foolish for doing this, as if the hat he always wore outside had somehow disguised his identity. "I'm Hank, Eliza." Saying this felt even more absurd.

Her eyes narrowed.

"Your husband," he added, although he spoke the last word with a slight upward inflection, almost like a question. *Your husband of 53 years,* he wanted to yell.

Her eyes grew wide, but her posture softened as a sliver of recognition took root.

Hank stepped forward and offered a hand. She looked at it carefully, like questioning if it was a trap. For the first time, he noticed she wheezed with every breath.

"C'mon dear, let's get you up." He avoided leaning too close.

Eliza slowly reached up and took his hand. Hank held it for a moment, then extended his other, which she also accepted. He stepped over her, girding himself, before pulling her onto her feet.

Eliza blinked repeatedly, eyeing her surroundings, while brushing herself off distractedly. She turned to him and examined him in silence. "My husband," she eventually repeated, as though she was managing to sort it all out.

He nodded. "And you're Eliza. My wife." He moved closer, and when she did not pull away, he wrapped an arm around her. "Let's go in our house now." He made a point of calling it *our* house—not *the* house.

He took a small stride forward, and she followed. Stepping over the knitting needle, he led her toward the barn door opening.

"Our house," she said, sort of turning the words over as she spoke them. She took in a sequence of shaky breaths as they traversed the backyard toward the farmhouse. "Hank. And Eliza."

When they crossed the back porch and Hank reached out to pull open the screen door, Eliza asked, "What happened to me, Hank?"

Relieved she called him by his name, Hank led her inside. "I'm not sure, dear, but it's nothing to worry about." He wished he believed so.

Hank pulled up the kitchen chair that had been knocked over and slid it under the table. "Let's go into the parlor."

Beyond the kitchen, they passed the dining room with four place settings arranged on the table. As they approached the parlor, Hank glimpsed an old man, reflected in the pier mirror mounted beside the front door. His grandmother had once told him how, when she looked in the mirror, she was surprised to see an old woman staring back. Hank had laughed at the time, but now found himself able to relate to the sentiment.

A few steps further, and they entered the parlor, finding the room in shambles. They both halted and gawked. The floor lamp had fallen, its globe shattered. The knitting bag had been dumped, its contents spilled across the rug. In the middle of the floor sat the skein, its yarn unspooled across the room, the lone needle sitting atop the connected tangle beside Eliza's knitting chair. She blinked, cocked her head, and asked, "Did I do this?" as though he might be able to provide an explanation.

Hank shrugged in his most casual way, swallowed, and said, "You sit on the couch, Eliza, while I pick this up."

CHAPTER 4

---◆◇◆---

DEATH SENTENCE

JULY 1, 2002

THREE RAPID KNOCKS, THEN the door swung ajar. "Mr. and Mrs. Mitchell?" Like an emerging tortoise, a head popped through the opening.

When Hank saw the expression on the general practitioner's face, his heart sank. This was not the look of a good-news-bearer.

"Come in, Doctor Powers," Eliza said cheerily, despite having been subjected to a wide array of tests during the six hours they had spent at the hospital.

Maybe she didn't notice his expression, Hank thought. But more likely, it was Eliza's maddening tendency to take everything in stride. *It's her Amish upbringing.* Although Eliza left the Amish when she was seventeen, their fatalistic outlook had already taken hold, and she never shook it.

Handsome but lanky, Doctor Jeff Powers stepped into the room, shaking both of their hands in a business-like way. He went to the counter and laid out his files. As he pored over each document, arranging them in some sort of order, Hank noticed large flakes of dandruff sprinkled amongst the man's black, wiry hair. He resisted the urge to look for more on the shoulders and collar of the physician's lab coat. Against the white cloth, it would have been an arduous search, anyway.

Doctor Powers straightened his back and pivoted around to face them. He let out an almost undetectable sigh. "There's no easy way to say this…"

Hank reached out and took Eliza's hand. She gave him a quick smile, raising her eyebrows in anticipation of the report, showing no outward sign of worry. Even her hand felt calm. Hank felt the urge to take his own hand back to wipe it dry.

"Mrs. Mitchell, you have stage four breast cancer."

The room fell silent. Doctor Powers peeled his eye contact away from Eliza, cast a glance at the floor, then to Hank, and back to the floor.

Eventually, Hank and Eliza asked in synchronized tandem, "Breast cancer?"

The physician frowned and nodded. He took a step backward and reclined against the counter, crossing his arms over his chest. "Often, patients don't know they have breast cancer until it's too late."

"Too late?" Hank felt his eyes stretching open. "Too late for what?"

"Too late to treat."

Hank stared at the doctor, searching for a clue of understanding. An image formed in his mind of Eliza when he first met her. Eighteen years old, working at the grain operation office, less than one year after leaving the Amish. Young, vibrant, and so healthy, this moment would seem impossible.

Doctor Powers sighed. "This recent episode occurred because the cancer has metastasized to the brain."

Hank's heart pounded like a sledgehammer, but Eliza just sat there, showing no emotion—like she had just been told it was time for lunch. "Metas...?" Hank started to ask, stumbling on the word.

"Stage four is metastatic cancer, which means the cancer has spread. It's in the brain now." He turned to Eliza. "This is the first episode you've experienced like this?"

She scrunched her nose and thought for a few seconds. "I've been getting confused at times, and...well, feeling out of sorts."

The physician nodded solemnly. "The radiologist found eight masses, spread across multiple lobes of your brain. To be honest, you seem to be doing better than I would have expected under the circumstances."

Hank studied him, at a loss for words.

"In addition, the cancer has spread to the lungs."

"The lungs?" Eliza said.

Doctor Powers pushed himself away from the counter and stood straight, nodding. "Have you noticed any shortness of breath or wheezing?"

Eliza furrowed her brow. "Well... yes, but it's not bad."

"The cancer in the lungs is not as advanced."

"So, what do we do?" Hank said, suddenly feeling light-headed. He tightened his grasp on Eliza's hand.

She squeezed his hand in return.

The physician shook his head grimly. "Realistically, the cancer in the brain is too advanced to treat. The psychoti—" He cut himself off and reconsidered his choice of words for a few seconds before starting over. "The *delusion* episode you experienced last week probably won't be a one-off incident."

Psychotic. The word the doctor had started to use caught Hank off guard, although he could not deny it seemed fitting.

"It's likely you'll have more confusion spells until..."

Doctor Powers's trailed-off response hung suspended over the room for what felt like forever.

"Until what?" Hank heard himself say through a choking sensation.

"What I'm saying is...there are limits to what we can treat. I'm sorry, but Mrs. Mitchell, your condition is terminal."

"Terminal." Thrown off by the word, Hank mumbled it, as if voicing the word might help him come to grips with it.

A swooning sensation overtook him, and his knees weakened. He let go of Eliza's hand and grabbed the edge of the examination table. The doctor stepped to the corner, pulled a chair out, and slid it toward Hank. He sat. His hands fumbled for his hat, which he felt an impulse to wring, but he'd left it in the truck.

"Terminal," he mumbled again. He turned his eyes to Eliza, who was watching him. She reached out for his hand again, like *she* was comforting *him*.

Terminal. The very word was so uncompromising, meaning there was no hope for an alternative outcome.

Doctor Powers pivoted back to the counter and slid open one of the drawers. He removed a card and held it out. Eliza did not move for it, so Hank took it, holding it so they could both could read it. The words at the top dispensed another gut punch:

Hospice of Homer County

"Oh, Hank," Eliza said, frowning, as though it was him she was concerned for.

"Hospice?" Hank asked, having a vague but clear enough understanding of what hospice entailed.

The physician nodded. "I'm referring you to their palliative care practice."

"Wait... how much time are we talking?"

Doctor Powers hesitated. "Every case is unique, so it's hard to predict. My best guess would be six months."

"Six months," Hank repeated slowly, subconsciously paging through the calendar. *The dead of winter.*

Hank felt a stabbing sensation in his chest. When he looked into Eliza's eyes, she gave little reaction. *Of course. Fatalism.* He turned back to the doctor. "*Six months?*"

"It could be longer, but it could be shorter. You'll want to get your affairs in order, Mrs. Mitchell. Then, it's a matter of making you comfortable. Episodes like the one you experienced will probably reoccur. They'll likely become more frequent. And worsen."

Worsen? Hank thought back to the nightmare incident from the week prior, of which Eliza had little recollection, and he wondered how it could have been any worse.

"I understand this isn't easy to take in. I encourage you to talk to the hospice center sooner rather than later. They're wonderful." Doctor Powers closed his notebook, signaling he was preparing to move on to another patient—one he could actually help. He patted Hank on the shoulder awkwardly, like this was a bedside mannerism he had been taught, but never really mastered.

Hank inhaled a trembling breath and tried to clear his throat.

Terminal. Six months. Worse yet, what would the six months be like for Eliza?

CHAPTER 5

CEMETERY

JULY 4, 2002

H ANK MET ELIZA BESIDE the barn, at the entrance to their family cemetery plot.

"Oh, those are pretty," she said, taking the wildflower bunch he had picked from his hand. She brought them to her nose, sniffed, and managed a meager smile. Her other hand clutched the familiar framed photo.

"Purple Coneflower and Black-eyed Susan," Hank said. "First blooms of the season." He'd collected them from the former garden patch on the opposite side of the barn. When they had quit growing their own produce, Eliza had scattered wildflower seeds over the cultivated soil and the native flowers flourished in the fertile ground.

"She would have loved them." Eliza pressed the bouquet against her chest and turned to the wrought iron entrance gate.

Hank unlatched and swung open the gate, its rusting hinges screeching as it swiveled. He removed his hat, and they both edged inside.

The family plot had been created by Hank's great-grandfather when he buried his father there in 1888. In all, the headstones of seventeen family members, spanning six generations, occupied the small plot. Simple sandstone markers topped the older graves, their carved lettering barely legible after decades of weathering, steadily fading away like lost memories. The newer headstones were made of granite, which held up to the harsh Ohio winters. Wrought iron fencing enclosed the back, front, and one side of the graveyard, while the side of the barn towered over the opposite flank.

Hank's throat tightened when they passed his brother's grave. Jimmy had been mortally wounded shortly after his overseas deployment during World War II, less than one year after reporting for basic training. Ma had left a place setting on the dining room table for him when he shipped out. He arrived home unable to walk, with a shrapnel souvenir embedded in his spine. Two weeks later, Jimmy was dead. Ma never did remove his dining room place setting; it remained, to this day. The war was over within months of Jimmy's passing, just as Hank himself was preparing to deploy for basic training.

Just beyond, they passed Ma and Pop's graves. Ma had added a dining room place setting for Pop after his heart had given out planting soybeans one spring. Just a few years later, Hank and Eliza had arranged Ma's place setting, making it three.

A few steps further, and they drew in on the newest grave marker.

"Oh, darling." Eliza reached out to touch the granite.

"Thirty years today," Hank said, his voice cracking. He traced the carved letters with his fingertips as if reading braille:

Brenda Sue Mitchell
Our Precious Daughter
January 30, 1954 – July 4, 1972

The fourth dining table place setting was Brenda's.

Hank pivoted around and stared across the backyard at the rear of the farmhouse, and the memory of it all came flooding back.

Brenda had come downstairs wearing her favorite pair of bell-bottom Levi's and a green summer top with "Sweet Pea" written on the front, the letters packed into a pea pod graphic.

"I'm not real hungry today," she had said as she settled at the kitchen table. She placed a single strip of roasted zucchini on her plate and reached over to the platter of chicken. "One leggy peg will do for me." She finger-tweezed a chicken leg and moved it to her plate.

The corners of Hank's mouth turned upward when her quirky word sunk in.

"Pass the puh-too-tees, please," Brenda said to her mother, over-enunciating each syllable.

Hank's smile widened as he shook his head. How Brenda invented such fanciful words was a mystery to him, but she had developed a real knack for it.

Eliza's face mirrored Hank's smile as she handed her daughter the bowl of mashed potatoes. "Saving room for that junky fair food?"

"Elephant ears aren't junky," Brenda responded with feigned indignation. She had always been partial to the fried dough, sprinkled with powdered sugar.

The lacy curtains above the sink billowed into the kitchen on a hot breeze, flooding the table with late-day sunshine. Hank, determined to remain a spectator in the exchange, squinted as the light reflected off the table.

"You really should eat more." Eliza turned and gave Hank a subtle shrug.

"I'm late." Brenda shoveled what was left of the mashed puh-too-tees into her mouth. "Kathy's expecting me at six. We want to get to Clarkton by 6:30."

"The fireworks don't start until ten," Eliza pointed out.

Brenda bit into the last chunk of chicken and peeled it off the bone. "Mom, everyone's probably there already," she said with a half-full mouth. It was their summer after high school graduation. In two months, Brenda and Kathy were to become roommates at The Ohio State University Agricultural Institute. Only one of them would make it.

"Did you water your pumpkins?" Hank asked. He had allocated a small corner of his field for a pumpkin patch, Brenda's first attempt at growing the winter squash. Pumpkins needed a lot of water if you wanted them to grow big, but they had been in a dry spell.

"I sure did." Brenda stood and carried her dishes to the sink. "Took me over an hour to haul all that water."

"Home by midnight," Eliza said.

"I know." Brenda grabbed the keyring from the hook near the door and made a dramatic show of blowing a kiss. She flung the back screen door open, and called over her shoulder, "Bye. Love you!"

"Love you!" Hank and Eliza responded in unison as Brenda bounded out toward Hank's pickup truck.

Darkness had fallen. Hank was wrapping up a couple of chores in the barn shortly after ten o'clock when a vehicle's tires came crunching along the gravel roadway, slowing near the house, then pulling into the drive. *That's strange,* he'd thought, *It's nowhere near midnight.*

He leaned over the workbench through a swarm of insects fluttering around the overhead lights and flicked off the switch, enveloping himself in blackness. With the path illuminated only in his mind by a lifetime of familiarity, he skirted toward the barn's man door through the darkened maze. When he stepped outside and recognized the sheriff's Plymouth Fury behind the headlights, his heart began to race.

Hank started across the lawn toward the car, while the sheriff stepped out and made for the back door. The porch lamp cast just enough light to illuminate a somber look plastered on the sheriff's face.

In the thirty years since, Hank would always remember observing the rhythmic pulsing of hundreds of lightening bugs throughout the reaches of his yard and beyond, as he walked from the barn toward the house. The hypnotic and almost magical display of a proliferation of fireflies blinking in the darkness, each beckoning a mate, would endure as a fragment of his recollection of that dreadful evening.

When Hank passed the wishing well, Eliza emerged from the rear door. All three of them would convene behind the farmhouse at just about the same moment. As he approached the back portico, the sheriff removed his campaign hat and held it against his chest. Gasping when she saw him do this, Eliza grabbed the door frame to stabilize herself.

Hank reached for Eliza as he stepped with watery legs onto the sandstone slab tucked outside the rear door. A swarm of moths fluttered around them, dancing haphazardly under the porch light, contributing to his disorientation. Hank swallowed and forced himself to breathe, while Eliza trembled under his arm.

"Folks, I'm Sheriff Roger Miller."

Eliza let out an audible moan.

"I'm so sorry," the sheriff said, staring at a spot on the stoop between them. "Brenda's truck slid off Township Road 108 and rolled into the gully."

As if she somehow knew there was no point even asking if Brenda was okay, Eliza wailed and leaned into Hank, wrapping her arms around him.

Sheriff Miller's next three words plunged a dagger into their hearts.

"She didn't suffer." Hank voiced the sheriff's words out loud, startling himself, and time skipped forward thirty years, snapping him back into the moment.

She didn't suffer. A hollow consolation, but it *was* something.

A half step behind him, Eliza let out a sob. Hank turned around and watched as she nudged forward and set the photo on top of Brenda's headstone, then slowly rearranged the clutch of wildflowers while tears spilled down her cheeks. Closing her eyes, she pressed the bouquet against her nose and took in a deep sniff, like savoring the scent along with the memories of her lost daughter, who, as a child, would forage around the property for the same striking purple and yellow flowers.

"She would have loved them." After echoing her earlier comment, Eliza crouched and laid the bunch at the base of Brenda's grave marker. She rose, then placed both hands against the headstone, and while her body listed, she began to weep.

Hank clenched his teeth as he stepped beside and wrapped his arm around his wife, gently propping her upright. With his free hand, he lifted the frame and folded out the stand. Mother and daughter, smiling, tilting into each other, both wearing their equestrian outfits. The photo had been taken at the Homer County Dressage Competition less than a month before Brenda's death.

"Three decades now," Hank said with teary eyes. "It never gets easier, does it?"

Eliza shook her head. "I miss our baby." Her voice choked out, and she covered her mouth with her hand.

Hank pulled her against his body and felt her twitching as she cried.

"I miss…" Eliza blinked, lifting her eyes to gaze at the cornfield beyond the cemetery. "I miss…" She squinted as if she was working something out in her mind, then, after a long moment, turned to Hank. "Why can't I remember our baby's name?"

CHAPTER 6

MERCY KILLING

JULY 22, 2002

H ANK NOTICED HIS WIFE'S wheezing had worsened to a rasp when she stepped up beside him at the deli counter.

"What can I get you?" the girl asked as she met them from the opposite side. Her plain lavender dress with a subtle floral print and the thin white head covering gave her away as a Mennonite. In Homer County, Amish girls wore solid color dresses—often blue.

"We'll have two large sandwiches," Hank answered, saving Eliza the effort. "Ham and Swiss on one, turkey and cheddar on the other."

The girl nodded, scratched out a note, and went to work on the order.

They were at the Bretzler IGA, catching an early lunch before grocery shopping, on their way to meet with the hospice center. "Do you want to save us a table?" Hank asked.

Eliza scoffed, glancing over her shoulder at the half-dozen tables and the row of vacant booths, all empty. "There's no one else here."

"Right. But you might get another dizzy spell," Hank said. Eliza had experienced half a dozen such episodes in the two weeks since Doctor Powers had given them the tragic news, and during one, she had fallen in the kitchen. Luckily, she had not been hurt. And even more fortunately, aside from periods of forgetfulness and confusion, there had been no other "psychotic" episodes, as Doctor Powers had almost called them. Not yet, at least.

"I'm fine," Eliza said, averting eye contact.

Hank puckered his lips to the side but let it go. He opened his can of Dr Pepper and took a swig, then checked his watch and saw it was just after eleven o'clock. "I think we're going to be early."

"Of course," she said with a smile. "We were always late before you retired. Now we're always early. We'll eat and shop slowly." Eliza took gulps of breath between every couple of words, giving her speech a halting cadence.

After the girl handed them their sandwiches and rang them up, they settled into one of the booths. Hank opened Eliza's can of Sprite.

Eliza lifted the can to her lips, and as she swallowed her sip, she tossed her chin in the direction behind him. "They put up a new sign."

Hank twisted around and studied the painted wooden banner hanging above the menu, which read "The Carpenter's Diner." It was the same sign they had always had, probably since the IGA had opened in the 1970s. Yet Eliza had somehow forgotten it. "Yeah, that's a fancy sign," he said as he pivoted back around.

Eliza nodded slowly, squinting. "The 't' in 'carpenter' is a cross."

As he chewed a bite of his turkey and cheddar, Hank turned for another gander. She was correct: the "t" depicted a cross. He had probably seen the sign a hundred times, but he'd never noticed this detail. *It took fresh eyes,* he figured. "I reckon you're right." When the Mennonite girl gave him a questioning look, he rotated away.

"I suppose Jesus is the carpenter." Eliza gave a little smirk and shook her head. "Mennonites..."

Hank knew her feelings on the matter. Eliza had been raised Amish, but the day before her baptism, she had made the life-changing decision to leave. Her family and community shunned her, so she'd lived in complete seclusion from her former Amish circle ever since. Being shunned had left Eliza with emotional trauma that would stick with her for life. So naturally, she had strong opinions on the Amish ways. Her feelings did not carry over to the Mennonites, who did not practice shunning. Yet she always rolled her eyes at the Mennonite's evangelical habits. While the Amish considered themselves to be in an exclusive club, the Mennonites were always spreading the word to anyone who would listen, and at times, even those who would not.

"They're always slipping Jesus into everything," Eliza said with a chuckle, while she tucked her sandwich back into the wrapper. She had eaten less than half, but apparently, she was done.

"Seems like a stretch to me," Hank said, taking one more look over his shoulder at the sign. "I would never have noticed that cross if you hadn't pointed it out." He shrugged apologetically, as if their efforts had been wasted on him.

"I reckon working that symbol in made them feel better anyway," Eliza said, giving Hank a wink.

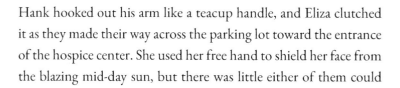

Hank hooked out his arm like a teacup handle, and Eliza clutched it as they made their way across the parking lot toward the entrance of the hospice center. She used her free hand to shield her face from the blazing mid-day sun, but there was little either of them could do about the heat radiating from the blacktop underfoot, which seemed to accentuate the emotional stress of their grim visit by adding an element of physical discomfort.

"Good afternoon, folks," the silver-haired receptionist, wearing an oversized string of pearls, said as they entered the air-conditioned interior. "Can I help you?"

"We have a one o'clock appointment with Tammy," Hank said, removing the sweat-moistened cap from his head. The clock on the wall read 12:45. "We're a bit early."

"Well, that's fine. Tammy takes her lunch early. I know she's expecting you." She rose and peered down the hallway to a cluster of offices. Hank figured the receptionist must have been a bored widow, volunteering to fill her days. She appeared older than him. But then again, he had realized long ago he often thought people looked older than him who actually weren't, and he'd concluded he probably didn't have a good sense of how old he looked to others, either.

The presumed widow wandered into the hallway, saying over her shoulder, "Please, have a seat." She gestured to the waiting area as an afterthought.

No sooner had they settled in the lobby chairs, than the receptionist returned with a chubby middle-aged woman carrying a clipboard.

"Welcome, Mr. and Mrs. Mitchell," the new arrival said between gum chews, and she reached out to shake each of their hands. "I'm Tammy. Please, come in."

Eliza reattached herself to Hank's arm, and they followed Tammy under the unnatural glare of fluorescent tubes lighting the opposite corridor. Some harsh scent thickened as they proceeded down the hall, which reminded Hank of moth balls...*mingled with remnants of...what?* The word "decay" came to mind. The place certainly appeared clean—almost sterile, like everything had been disinfected. They obviously tried to make it nice, but there was no covering up the fact that this was a place where people go to die. Eliza covered her nose with her fingers.

Tammy said, "I'd like to start by showing you one of our patient rooms."

Eliza stopped in her tracks. "Patient rooms? But we're interested in your in-home service."

Tammy held up and turned, placing the clipboard across the front of her pudgy torso, and gave a regretful smile. "We only provide in-home hospice care within a ten-mile radius of Clarkton's town square." She rotated the clipboard down and took a peek. "You live on Township Road 223, right?"

"Yes ma'am," Hank answered while wringing his hat. It had been he who had said so when he called to schedule the appointment after Eliza finally relented.

Tammy frowned sympathetically. "That's twenty-five miles from Clarkton."

Someone moaned in the nearby room. Hank pivoted and caught the sight of an elderly woman, her back toward them, stooped over an occupied bed. A strained, rattling inhale followed.

He pried his gaze away. Tammy motioned them onward. Before he complied, he turned to Eliza, who was staring into the room, eyes wide. He took a pace forward, giving her a gentle tug through their linked arms.

Tammy waddled to the end of the hall, stopping under a humming fluorescent bulb flickering above an open door. "This room is vacant right now." She gestured for them to enter.

Hank stepped aside for Eliza, but she held up. Tilting forward slightly, she glanced in, then leaned away. She gave a quick look at Hank, and her lower lip began to quiver. He slipped his arm around her and turned to face Tammy. "Do you ever make exceptions to this mileage limit?"

She sighed and shielded the middle of her bosom with the clipboard once again. "I wish we could, but not at our current staffing levels. This policy is the only way we can manage." Tammy turned to Eliza. "We strive to make it comfortable here. Would you like to have a better look inside?"

Eliza took in a deep, wheezing breath and bit her lower lip.

"Not right now," Hank said. "But you have a nice facility, Ma'am. We appreciate your time."

⚫

Hank held the pickup door open for Eliza, who needed a minute to catch her breath before climbing into the sweltering cab. Despite having left the windows open, the door panel was so hot he could barely touch it.

"I know it's not what you want," he said as he slid behind the wheel.

"No," Eliza said. She stretched the seatbelt over her, but before snapping the buckle in place, she hissed and yanked away her fingers.

Hank reached over and engaged her searing buckle, then clicked in his own. Without ever having discussed it, both of them had begun wearing seatbelts unfailingly after the Sheriff told them Brenda probably would have survived if she had been wearing hers.

He started the truck. Unfortunately, the air conditioning had quit working years earlier, but Hank turned the blower fan up to its highest setting and pointed the middle vents toward Eliza. She stared forward out the windshield for a moment with her lip quivering once again, before bursting into tears.

As Hank fought back his own tears, he pulled a handkerchief from his pocket and handed it to her. He left his palm open, and when she finished wiping her eyes, she took his hand.

"Please don't take me to die in a place like that," she said, clutching the hankie in her other hand, pressing it against her mouth.

Blinking, Hank squeezed her palm.

"I accept it's my time, Hank."

He nodded slowly and continued blinking.

"But please...let me die at home."

They were heading down the hill on Township Road 223, approaching the last bend in the gravel roadway at the eastern end of their property. Hank knew exactly how fast he could go without skidding on the loose stone at the turn. He made a point of braking more than he would have if Eliza had not been with him, but Eliza still said it.

"Careful, Hank."

His speed on the gravel surface was not the problem.

Seconds later, a flash raced across his peripheral vision, and Eliza shrieked. By the time he slammed on the brakes, the fender had already made impact with the deer. The pickup skidded before coming to a stop. A cloud of dust drifted forward, enveloping the truck.

Eliza buried her face in her hands.

With his heart thumping, Hank took in a sharp, hitching breath. He craned his neck but saw no deer through the dust. As the haze thinned, the ruins of Shirley Gould's farmhouse appeared, looming on the slope above them, like an ill omen.

"Ghoul House," as the kids had been calling it. A silent witness.

"Did you kill it?" Eliza said from under her palms, her fingers stretched over her eyes.

"I don't know." Hank put the truck in park, unbuckled his seat belt, pushed open his door, and slipped out. As he walked to the back end of the vehicle, the dust began to clear.

There, over the tailgate, the deer lay in the opposite ditch, panic flaring in its eyes. A young buck, with traces of late-summer velvet still covering fresh antlers. The animal struggled to pull himself upright, using his front legs only. Hank held back, keeping a distance to avoid frightening him further.

"I'm sorry," Hank said to the deer, and he covered his mouth with his palm.

The creature looked at him and huffed. He attempted to right himself, but soon crumpled back into the ditch. Then he tried again, with the same result.

Hank cringed under his palm and began backing away.

When he climbed into the truck, Eliza was still hiding behind her fingers, sobbing.

"Is it okay?"

Hank stared at his hands as he wrung them together, deliberating whether he should lie. With a slow shake of his head, he mouthed the word *no*.

Eliza whimpered.

"It's a buck. He's crippled. I'm going to take you to the house and get the rifle."

She nodded.

Eliza kept her eyes covered as Hank drove the last thousand feet before pulling into their driveway.

"Just leave the groceries, dear," he said as he put the gearshift in park. He had packed the refrigerated items in the cooler along with a bag of ice, so there was no need to hurry in moving them. "I'll get them when I return."

She uncovered her face and went about wiping her eyes and cheeks dry with his handkerchief before passing it back to him. Hank removed the clean new John Deere hat he had worn on the outing and held it out to her. "Take this into the house, please?"

She took the cap. "I'll wait in the parlor," she said softly before climbing out of the cab.

Hank plucked his mangy working hat (same logo, but a different size) from the floor's center hump console, pulled it onto his head, and slid out.

As he hurried to the barn, he wondered if a .22 would be enough firepower to kill a deer. It was all he had. A bullet in the heart would do it, he was sure. But Hank had never been a hunter, so he did not know enough about the animal's anatomy to pinpoint where that would be. The brain was the logical alternative, and there was no doubt where that was located. He should be able to get off a clean shot at point-blank range. *Better get it right, Old Man,* he thought.

He retrieved the rifle from the cabinet beside his workbench. After double-checking to confirm it was loaded, he set off and was soon panting while he trekked in the summer heat.

As he proceeded down the gravel roadway, peeks of the Gould farmhouse began poking through the greenery. When he was halfway there, he slowed his pace to avoid spooking the buck.

A crow cawed from the treetops across the gravel roadway, causing Hank to flinch. The sound brought back memories of his youth.

He and Jimmy often played in the Salem Creek, which ran along the roadway. For some reason, crows tended to congregate in this stretch of creek-side woods near the Gould farmhouse. Their calls still carried an ominous sound to him.

Hank strained to spot the deer as he ventured down the road, but all he sensed was the thrum of cicadas all around him. Eventually, sighting the truck's skid tracks, he padded toward them, until he found the location in the ditch where the buck had fallen. The saddle of flattened weeds was now empty. Hank scanned his surroundings, knowing the animal could not have gone far.

Following along the berm of the roadway, he located signs of trampled flora. He leaped across the ditch, climbed the small embankment, and waded into the scrub, where he stopped to survey the scene.

There. Amid what had once been the front lawn of the Gould farmhouse, two black eyes glared out from a gap in the jumble of vegetation.

"It's okay, buddy," Hank heard himself say, although his quaking voice belied his words of reassurance.

The buck snorted and struggled upright, tottering on three legs. Clearly, one of its rear legs—or a hip—had been fractured. Through the years, Hank had seen plenty of maimed bucks, so he knew broken legs were not uncommon. Often, they were injured from being hit by a vehicle, and sometimes, fractures were sustained as collateral damage when rival males battled during rutting season. If they were not completely immobilized, a deer with a broken leg might manage to limp around for some time. But such cases eventually meant a slow and grueling winter starvation.

With a labored wheeze, the buck turned and hobbled in the opposite direction. After half a dozen steps, he collapsed near the gaping hole that had once been Shirley's front doorway, bleating as he dropped.

"Oh, geez," Hank whispered as he scuttled through the overgrowth, sidestepping patches of poison ivy blanketing the ground.

The buck made one more attempt to rise, but fell in vain into a heap, panting and writhing. With a hammering heart, Hank closed in on the lame creature, trying to swallow away what felt like a horse chestnut that had lodged in his throat.

Don't drag this out, Old Man, he told himself. *It ain't gonna get any easier.* He meandered through the weeds, stepping around the buck, taking the rifle in both hands while releasing the safety. The animal looked up at him with fearful eyes and blew out a heavy breath.

"I'm sorry," Hank said, raising the rifle and pointing it at the top of the buck's head. He drew in a sharp intake of air, held it, lined up the sights for a spot between and slightly in front of the antlers, and moved his finger to the trigger.

The creature's head rolled. Hank exhaled in a sigh. "I don't want to do this," he said under his breath, and when the deer stopped moving, he took aim once again.

The crack of the rifle shot echoed across the valley, sounding three or four times before fading to silence. A drove of crows scattered into the sky from the stand of trees across the road, and a startled buzzard took wing from the house.

The buck's head dropped, his eyelids sprung permanently open. A hole in the top of his head turned bright red. His body flinched, spasmed, then fell still.

Mercy killing. The words formed in Hank's mind as he blinked away a tear from the corner of his eye. He swung the rifle to one hand

and pulled the handkerchief, still damp from Eliza's use, out from his pocket.

Mercy killing.

Hank took two short backward paces and dropped to a sitting position on the sandstone step of the house. He wiped his eyes, watching for any signs of movement, regretting everything that had transpired, but finding solace in the knowledge that he'd made the best possible choice.

After the deer remained motionless for over a minute, Hank averted his gaze. He slid around, taking in the sight of the ruins of Shirley Gould's home.

According to Pop, the Cape Cod-style dwelling had been built by an early Ohio settler in the early 1820s. Despite over three-quarters of a century of abandonment, much of the external structure somehow remained upright. The opposite gable wall had buckled a decade or two earlier, leaving the caved-in roof pancaked onto the top floor.

Hank hauled himself to his feet. He peered into the splintered opening that had once been the front door. The scent of rot drifted out. Mounting the sandstone block, he leaned inside and waited for his eyes to adjust to the gloom.

A large portion of the floor had fallen into the cellar, leaving the surrounding sections cantilevering perilously in free space. In the corner, one lone wooden milk crate remained on the short stub of floor-ledge, and Hank wondered if it might contain the remnants of a certain Sears Catalog. As he pulled away and stepped off the stone doorstep, he half-heartedly smiled at the memory of him and his brother ogling the women's undergarment section.

Edging along the house, he picked his way through the tangles until he could see around the corner. The stacked sandstone foundation along that side had caved in, exposing a cleft of darkness. Fifty yards beyond the back corner lay the Gould family cemetery, now virtually hidden within the encroaching band of woods that had overtaken it.

Shirley Gould's empty grave had been filled when it became clear her remains would not be recovered. The case had never been solved, but this macabre development had certainly ratcheted up the home's infamous folklore, and, according to the stories Brenda had brought home, triggered fresh yarns involving Shirley as a zombie.

A few years after Shirley's interred corpse had gone missing, Pop bought the neighboring four-acre Gould property when it went into foreclosure, consolidating it into the Mitchell farm. Hank and Jimmy had protested when they learned of the purchase, but it was too late; the deal had already closed. *Course, it's yours now, Old Man,* Hank reminded himself, turning away from the cloistered family plot with one eternally vacant grave.

Better check on Eliza. He retraced the path he had trampled through the overgrowth, along the house, and back to where the buck lay. As he drew in on the carcass, he instinctively pulled his hat from his head, holding it against his chest. "I'm sorry," Hank said once again.

A couple of flies buzzed around the oozing red dot. He questioned whether he should attempt to drag the poor creature to the edge of the woods, but decided it would be too difficult. *I could get the tractor,* he thought. But he soon dismissed the idea, figuring it made no difference.

A shadow swept by. Hank tilted his head back and raised his eyes. A buzzard circled above, perhaps the latest in countless generations of turkey vultures that had nested in the old house, returning every one of the past 66 years. Orbiting. Anticipating its home, or a meal—or both.

Hank Mitchell pulled the cap back on his head, stepped around the carcass, and set off for home, allowing nature to take its course.

CHAPTER 7

UNDER SIEGE

AUGUST 19, 2002

THE FRONT WALKWAY'S FIRST sandstone slab had shed a wide chunk of stone long ago, leaving a two-inch deep crater across much of its surface. "The rain gauge," Pop had called it.

Hank watched the rain gauge, assessing the frequency and size of the still-falling raindrops in the brimming puddle. "I think it's finally letting up."

"Seems so," Eliza said, pausing from her knitting to examine the drops falling from the roof on one side of the porch. "It was a good rain."

Hank nodded and took a swig from his can of Dr Pepper. "A fine soaking, no runoff. A farmer's rain." Although he had retired a few years earlier and now leased their roughly one-hundred-acre field to another farmer, he still thought like one himself.

The steady drizzle had lasted much of the day, unusual for late summer in Ohio, where rain this time of year normally came in short, heavy bursts via quick passing fronts.

"Sitting out here while it's raining...it's one of my favorite things," Eliza said wistfully, as though she understood there would not be many more chances.

There was a crash in the distance, the familiar sound of one of the buzzard parents landing on the tin roof of Shirley Gould's ruined farmhouse.

"Welcome home, Mama-bird," Hank said.

"Maybe it's Papa," Eliza pointed out.

"Yeah, could be." Buzzards mated for life, often returning to the same nesting site, and both parents would tend the nest and raise the hatchlings together. While this season's offspring had likely fledged by now, the family would stick around until late September, when they would depart on their winter migration south.

Hank and Eliza had settled in after lunch. Hank took roost on the porch swing, alone, while Eliza sat on the metal patio chair he had brought up from the backyard, the oxygen tank on the floor beside her. Lately, she had been keeping the tank with her, at the ready for when she experienced what the palliative care nurse called "air hunger."

A clattering sound arose over the patter of rain. Hank swung around and cocked his head. It was the crunch of gravel, yet too weak to be a car. He put his can of pop on the floor and stood, gaping at the bend in the roadway just beyond Shirley Gould's house.

It was Eliza who put a name to it. "A horse and buggy? Here?"

Hank rubbed the back of his neck, watching a chocolate-colored horse emerge, followed by a black buggy. He turned to Eliza. She had paused her knitting once again and gone stiff, her eyes widening. The unresolved trauma of being shunned still caused her to withdraw when the Amish were around. She lived in perpetual fear of coming face-to-face with one of the individuals who had shunned her, despite living in opposite corners of the county and never having experienced a random run-in throughout the 55 years since she left. Hank always sympathized with Eliza for the pain she had endured and never overcame, but while he did not understand why many Amish practiced shunning, who was he to question their culture?

"What's an Amish buggy doing on this road?" she asked, placing her knitting in the bag beside her, opposite the oxygen.

"Got me." Hank went on rubbing his neck. These days, Township Road 223 had only five active residences along its four-and-a-half-mile stretch through the Salem Valley, none of which were Amish households. While Homer County was heavily populated with Amish, they were mostly concentrated in the northeastern corner of the county, and the Amish rarely ventured far from home. Come to think of it, he could not remember *ever* seeing an Amish traveler on this roadway.

As the buggy drew closer, a lone occupant angled forward into view. The bearded young man, which indicated he was married, raised his hand in a still, tentative wave.

Hank returned the raised hand gesture.

When the buggy reached the driveway, the Amishman pulled back on the reins, and the horse came to a stop.

"You can go inside if you want," Hank said to Eliza.

She sighed as she mulled this over, then shook her head. "I'll stay here."

He stepped off the porch and descended the stairs to the sandstone walkway. As he sidestepped the rain gauge, he noted the drizzle had almost tapered off completely.

The Amishman climbed out of the buggy, holding the reins, as Hank turned onto the gravel drive.

"I wanted to introduce myself," the visitor called from the end of the drive. With no hitching post, he held up near his horse. "I'm going to be your new neighbor."

Neighbor? Hank looked back at Eliza. She gave no reaction, so he judged she was out of earshot.

"That so?" Hank said, nearing the end of his driveway.

"I'm Levi Hostetler," the Amishman said as Hank approached, reaching out to offer a handshake.

Hank shook the man's hand. "You're moving here?"

"Sure am. Two of my brothers and I bought a piece of property about half a mile down the road. We're starting a new settlement."

Hank looked that way, measuring the distance in his mind. "That empty cabin beside the road?"

"That's right."

"You're not moving into that cabin, though, are you?"

Levi squinched his face into a scoff. "I don't think that cabin would be very nice to live in."

"No, I reckon not. We used to call it Hillbilly Cabin."

Levi arched his eyebrows.

"That place was ramshackle even when The Hillbillies were living there. One night, they had a fire. Heck, must have been fifty years ago now. They left in their pajamas and never returned. The place has sat empty ever since."

Levi scratched his beard. "How long have you lived here?"

"I was born in this house." Hank paused to check his math. "Seventy-four years."

"Hmmm." Levi gave a look of surprise. "I wouldn't have guessed you're that old."

Hank just smiled. He heard this from time to time and was proud of how well he had aged. While his body tended to feel a bit creaky and stiff at times, he remained strong and had no chronic pains. He took no medications, although truth be told, he was so long overdue for a checkup he was now afraid to go. Aside from his thinning hair and declining eyesight, he still felt like the same old Hank Mitchell, although the emphasis shifted to the word "old" as the rest of humanity kept getting younger in comparison. The days of his youth, when he was always trying to keep up with his big brother, seemed like a past life now. "You'll get there too someday."

Levi chuckled and added, "If I'm lucky." He patted his horse. "Anyway, what's left of that cabin will be demolished in a few weeks."

Hank shifted his weight to his other leg. "You're building a new house?"

Levi nodded. "Three of them. The property is only eight acres, but we figure that's enough for our three families. We'll start building before the end of September. You're going to see quite a few of us coming through here."

Hank considered this. It was not as if *he* had a problem with having Amish in the proximate area, but this would be tough on Eliza. She did not exactly have a *problem* with the Amish; she just needed distance from them. They were a tight-knit group, and her hurt ran deep. "Is your church district nearby?"

"We're forming a new church district for the settlement. My oldest brother will be the bishop. A couple other families will be joining us in the spring. They're buying land on Township Road 217." Levi pointed in the direction of the next gravel roadway to the south.

"I've been seeing more Amish in these parts," Hank said.

"Yup, we're overflowing in northeastern Homer County. It's hard to find land out there anymore. Expensive too."

Hank knew the Amish population was booming, so their geographic footprint was expanding. "It's all those kids you keep having."

Levi laughed and shrugged. "Not sure what causes that." He patted his horse again. "Well, Ginger, we'd better get on our way." Then he turned to Hank and added, "Looks like the rain let up just in time for me to walk the new property."

Hank extended his hand, and Levi gave him a firm handshake before climbing back into his buggy and shaking the reins. From the end of the driveway, Hank waited, watching as the buggy began to roll. Levi raised his hand in a departing wave, then slid back out of view as the buggy headed forth down the roadway.

Hank kept his eyes fixed on the driveway as he navigated around the puddles and patches of mud where the gravel had worn thin, all the while asking himself, *What do I say to Eliza?*

When he reached the sandstone walkway, she let out a heavy, strangled moan. Hank looked up at the porch and instantly recognized something was dreadfully wrong. Eliza's head tilted back, her face aimed at the ceiling, mouth ajar. Her entire body had stiffened, her legs locked straight out, toes pointing back toward her body. Her arms had gone rigid, hands twitching in her lap, fingers splayed open.

Hank froze as he tried to make sense of the situation. "Eliza?"

She merely spasmed.

His mind flashed back to the idea she was possessed. He swept the notion aside, broke free from his paralysis, and hurdled up the steps to her side. "Eliza!"

She gave a wet choking sound. Her eyes had rolled upward to the whites, leaving just a sliver of her blue irises visible between her lids.

Hank grabbed her hands. They shook, then relaxed, then shook again as her arms and legs began convulsing. She gurgled, and foaming spittle rose to her lips. Liquid streamed down from the seat, pooling on the floor underneath her, and he soon caught a pungent whiff of urine.

Her body rocked, wobbling the chair. He leaned against the seat's metal arm to stabilize it and realized her face was turning blue. The oxygen tank and mask lay on the floor beside her, untouched. He dropped to his knees, turned the valve open with shaking fingers, snatched the mask, and pressed it against her face. The convulsions began lessening as she gulped in the oxygen. Her body went limp, and her eyeballs slowly rolled back into their normal position.

Then, within seconds, perhaps the strangest thing yet happened: Eliza shut her eyes and began snoring under the oxygen mask.

My God, how can she be sleeping? Hank thought, his own heart ricocheting inside his chest. He wondered if he should rouse her. *She must need the rest,* he told himself. *Whatever happened to her...it must've worn her out.*

Watching for the slightest of twitches, he kept the mask against her face, feeling helpless that this was all he could do. Eliza never flinched. She just went on snoring as though she had fallen into the deepest slumber.

As time slowed to a crawl, Hank wrestled with the wisdom of letting her sleep. Was this really the best thing for her? Yet she looked so peaceful, he could not bring himself to wake her.

Gotta get her to the hospital. Hank knew calling an ambulance was not much of an option—the farm was too remote. The crew would likely have a tough time even finding the place since only locals knew the township roads. *If I drive fast, I could get there in little more than half an hour.*

He craned his neck and leered at his pickup truck, but felt paralyzed. *Just hold this oxygen mask and let her rest.*

After fifteen of the longest minutes he'd ever experienced, Eliza's snoring began tapering off, and before long, she started peeling her eyes open. Only when she started to blink and lift her head upright did he pull the mask away.

When she looked into his eyes, he said, "We need to get you to the hospital, dear."

Squinting, she regarded him before sitting up. "Why?"

Hank pulled back and studied her, attempting to discern whether she was clowning around.

Eliza panned her surroundings and then turned back to Hank. "What are we doing out here?"

———— ◆○◆ ————

The emergency room physician had no trouble tracking down Doctor Jeff Powers, who happened to be on call that afternoon.

"Hello again, Mr. and Mrs. Mitchell," Doctor Powers said as he stepped into the exam room, shaking hands with each of them. Hank immediately spotted the handsome but gangly man's dandruff and looked away.

Eliza smiled pleasantly.

"The ER doc filled me in," the doctor said, then, turning to Eliza, "We think you may have had a seizure."

"A seizure." Hank nodded slowly. Yes, what he'd witnessed *was* what he imagined a seizure might be like.

"Seizures are not uncommon in people with your condition. They're caused by the brain tumors."

"But what about that nap?" Hank asked.

"Yes, that probably seemed strange. But it's typical for certain types of seizures. It's what we call the postictal phase, and it's caused by cerebral blood flow effects and the impact on neurotransmitters."

Hank responded with a blank stare.

Eliza shrugged. "I don't remember a thing."

"That's not unusual either. Some memories of what happened may come back to you in time. But as a precaution, we'd like to admit you for observation. There are a few tests we'd like to run."

"Do you mean for the night?" Eliza gaped at him with raised eyebrows.

Hank knew she had not spent a night away from home since 1954 when she'd given birth to Brenda. He placed his hand on her shoulder.

Doctor Powers tapped his pen against his chin. "Most likely you'd go home tomorrow."

"Oh, I really don't think that's necessary," Eliza said.

Seeing the opportunity he'd been waiting for, Hank rubbed his wife's shoulder. "It can't hurt, dear."

CHAPTER 8

SANCTIMONY

AUGUST 20, 2002

H ANK FIDGETED IN THE chair like a schoolboy in the principal's office. At first, he'd been happy to have found the opportunity to come, since he could no longer leave Eliza alone at home. Her hospital stay had finally given him the chance. But now that he was here, he wished he was not.

Hank scanned the items in front of him on the desk, looking for something to occupy his mind. He studied a souvenir baseball with "Chief Wahoo" on it, the Cleveland Indians' mascot. Beside it sat another with a logo he did not recognize. He picked the ball up and examined the markings, learning it was the Akron Aeros minor league team.

Just then, Hank wondered if the pastor's office might be under video surveillance. He looked around but spotted no cameras. Regardless, he replaced the baseball with the strange dog-cat-thing logo on its stand. As he slid his fingers under his legs to trap them, the sound of footfalls arose behind him.

"Good morning, Hank," Lionel Burns said, giving a hearty smile as he walked into the room, hand outstretched.

"Hello, Reverend Burns." Hank stood, feeling a wave of misgivings about his visit. His mind groped for an out, and when it drew a blank, he regretted he had not armed himself with a backup plan. The men exchanged a handshake.

"Please, have a seat." The minister motioned to the chair Hank had just risen from while lowering himself into the seat behind his desk. Leaning back, he gave Hank a look—pleasant enough, yet also questioning.

He's wondering why I'm here. Why shouldn't he? I haven't exactly been around the Clarkton Baptist Church much since Brenda died.

"How's Eliza?"

The abrupt question caught Hank off guard. His mind spun, working out an answer. "Well..." Despite having played out the conversation in his head for weeks, all that mental preparation was failing him. *Get it together, Old Man.*

Hank finally managed to push a string of words out of his mouth. "Well, that's why I'm here."

The pastor showed no reaction.

"She ain't doing well. She's in the hospital right now."

A look of concern spread over Lionel Burns's face. *Or is that false concern?* Hank dropped his eyes. Maybe his skepticism was unfair.

"I'm sorry to hear that, Hank." The preacher waited, like expecting Hank to continue, then prompted him when he didn't. "Is there anything I can do?"

"No. She's real sick. Ca...Cancer." Hank sort of coughed out the word from his tightened throat. He picked his hat off the desk and began wiping the sweat from his palms onto the cap's band. With his gaze directed at the baseballs in front of him, he muttered, "It's gotten in her brain and her lungs."

Pastor Burns blew out a sigh. "She's being treated?"

Hank shook his head and took a sharp breath. "It's terminal." His voice croaked when he spoke the words. He turned and looked out the window at the playground, vaguely watching as two boys climbed the rusting dome structure, while a young woman, standing nearby, lit a cigarette.

"Oh, that's terrible news. I'm sorry." A long moment of silence followed. "How's Eliza dealing with it?"

Hank pulled himself back into the present and faced the minister. *This is it...now's the time, Old Man.*

"She ain't complaining, but she's scared. She's going downhill fast. It's like...she's losing her mind. And...she's having problems breathing." Hank tilted his head back and looked up at the ceiling. "And it's going to get worse."

"I'm sorry, Hank. You'll both be in my thoughts and prayers."

Thoughts and prayers.

Hank lowered his head and looked the pastor in the eye. "The thing is...Reverend Burns, I'm thinking...I'm going to need to end it for her."

The preacher flinched. He narrowed his eyes, and a vertical wrinkle formed between his eyebrows.

Hank felt a sudden swell of nausea. The revelation had tumbled out of his mouth like a reflex, surprising even himself when he heard it. This was not how he'd planned the conversation, but there was nothing he could do to retract what he'd said. Something in his lap shook, and he looked down to discover it was his cap, held in his trembling hands. He placed the hat on the desk but kept his eyes glued to it while he slid his fingers under his legs to keep them still. After an extended silence, Hank looked up.

Pastor Burns arched one eyebrow at Hank. At first, it looked like he was trying to make sure he understood what he had heard. Then, it was like he was giving Hank a chance to admit he was merely joking. When that did not happen, his face hardened. He took in a heavy breath, ran his hands through his hair, and exhaled audibly. "What do you mean?" As he awaited the explanation, he steepled his fingers and pressed them against his frowning lips.

Hank locked eyes with the minister. "She's only got a few months left. It's going to get bad for her. That's no way to live."

Lionel Burns's chair creaked as he pressed his weight backward while planting a probing stare on Hank. "But you can't do that."

"I can't let her suffer."

The pastor huffed and pitched forward. "That's not the Lord's way." His cheeks had gone rosy. "You must rid your mind of such evil thoughts." He spat the words as if sermonizing from the pulpit.

Hank sat back in his chair as the realization he would not find an ally in Pastor Burns sank in. How stupid was he for having imagined he might have?

"You've got to pray, Hank." Lionel Burns fell into a stern glower, practically shooting daggers from his pupils. "The Lord has given you this burden, and he will give you the strength to carry it."

As the words sank in, Hank's anger ratcheted up but veered away from himself. "It's not *me* I'm worried about! It's Eliza who's suffering—and she's going to die, anyway. What's the point of making her suffer? Why would the Lord want that?"

"We can't question God's ways, Hank. The Lord will give Eliza strength too."

Heat flared on Hank's face. He clenched his jaw and returned his eyes to his hat.

Both men went speechless for a long, uncomfortable stretch of time. Eventually, the pastor broke the silence. "Life's sacred, Hank. Taking someone's life...only God can do that."

Hank nodded as he returned his gaze to the playground, where one boy had reached the top and was declaring victory over the other. The woman tilted her head back and blew a plume of smoke into the air. Hank wondered: had he really expected the man's blessing?

"You'd burn in hell for performing the devil's work."

Divergent impulses swirled in Hank's mind as he looked back at the pastor. It was clear there could be no arguing with this man—there was no use even trying. But the part of him who said he needed to find a graceful way to end the discussion lost out to the part of him who said he just needed to leave. "I reckon you're right."

Reverend Burns's posture softened, and a smug look took hold on his face.

"Thanks for clearing that up." Hank's words slurred, his tongue feeling as though it had grown too large for his mouth.

The minister gave a questioning look as he watched Hank reach for his cap and then stand.

"I'd best get over to the hospital. They're supposed to release her later this morning."

Reverend Burns seemed caught off guard by the abrupt end of the discussion. "Can we talk again soon, Hank?"

Hank shrugged. "The thing is, I need to tend to Eliza now. But thanks for helping me see things right." He hesitated, then forced himself to reach across the desk and offer his hand.

They shook. The pastor studied Hank warily. "Remember, Hank: the devil's work."

CHAPTER 9

DOCTOR DEATH

SEPTEMBER 17, 2002

HANK MITCHELL WHEELED ELIZA to the foot of the stairs. Methodically, he set the brakes on both sides of the chair and helped lift her feet free of the footrests. She had not resisted switching to the wheelchair, although he knew how much she hated the idea of it. But between her shortness of breath and the increasingly frequent dizzy spells, she had little choice but to acquiesce.

She *had* refused the OxyContin Doctor Powers had prescribed, complaining she did not like the foggy feeling the painkiller gave her the single time she had tried it. Afterward, Hank had begun scheming to slip it into her food. He even went as far as to grind up a pill, blending the chalky residue in with her peanut butter. But before he spread it on her toast, he changed his mind and threw the concoction away.

Later that day, while Eliza had been sleeping, he called Doctor Powers to ask whether he should encourage her to take the pills. "It's all about her comfort, Hank. If the painkillers don't make her comfortable, she shouldn't take them." So much for that.

Hank held both hands out to Eliza. "I'll come back for the oxygen," he said, noticing how much her thighs had shriveled in the past month while she became less and less active.

She nodded, took his hands, and held on as he pulled her upright. Hank waited, ensuring she was stable on her spindly legs before releasing her hands.

He wrapped an arm around her waist and led her to the first stair-step. She reached for the banister and they began their ascent, one step at a time. Five risers in, Eliza began gasping, her body lurching at the transition from exhale to inhale.

The upstairs climbs had become their biggest ordeal yet in the steady progression of her illness. Before long, Hank would need to carry her. Even at 74 years of age, having held up well, he felt he could do it. But how would this be for Eliza?

"Let's stop here," he said.

She nodded, a rattle escaping her throat with each breath, sort of like the sound of a purring cat, but more ragged, phlegmier.

"Do you need oxygen?"

She hesitated with a strained expression, then shook her head. "I think I can manage."

Hank assessed the stairway and guessed they were only one-third of the way up. "I'll get it just in case."

Eliza gave a tiny shrug.

"You've got the banister?"

She grasped it with her second hand. Her dizzy spells came on without warning, as did the seizures, caused by the masses on her brain. Doctor Powers had explained Hank's role was to make sure Eliza did not hurt herself when a seizure came on. She'd had five more in the four weeks since the first horrible episode. Two had occurred within the past few days, which seemed to signal they were becoming more frequent.

He went back down to retrieve the oxygen tank from the wheelchair's pouch. He glanced at the level gauge; it was still over half full. She had been using more oxygen in the past week or two, but most of the time she tapped the larger tank kept in the parlor, mounted on a small dolly.

"Want a swig?" he asked when he returned to the fifth step.

She was sweating lightly, but said, "Not yet."

Since her labored breathing had diminished, he let it go. He cradled the tank in one arm and reattached his other around her waist.

They resumed their ascent. After five more stairs, Eliza's lungs were heaving. This time, Hank did not ask. With both of her hands latched onto the banister, he set the tank on the step above them, untangled the hose, opened the valve, and lifted the mask to her face. The color began returning to her cheeks.

"Five more steps," Hank said.

Eliza drew in another dose, followed it with an air breath, and handed him the mask. "That stuff's like a miracle drug."

He chuckled as he turned off the valve.

"I wish I weren't such a burden on you," Eliza said, her eyes downcast.

"Pfft." Hank tucked the tank back under his arm. "Don't be silly." Of course, if it had been him, that was exactly how he would be feeling. He slipped his arm back around her. "Ready?"

Eliza mounted the next tread in response. With her oxygen level boosted, she managed the rest of the way without another stop. When Hank paused at the top, she pressed on, saying, "I can keep going."

They continued toward the bedroom at the end of the hall, past and opposite his own. It had been Brenda's bedroom. Eliza had slept—or tried to sleep—there the very night Brenda had died, and she had never abandoned it since then. As Eliza's state worsened over the past three months, Hank had suggested moving her to the daybed downstairs, but even all these years later, she was unwilling to desert Brenda's room.

Hank snapped on the light. Eliza dropped into the rocking chair beside the bed to catch her breath again. He placed the mask on the nightstand and the tank on the floor underneath, then sat on the edge of the bed across from her.

The clock on the dresser ticked a steady rhythm, out of sync with Eliza's erratic wheeze.

Her knitting bag sat in the corner, cast aside. In recent weeks, she had begun complaining about how difficult her favorite pastime had become. "My fingers can't remember what to do, and my head gets all confused when it tries to help," she had said. It occurred to Hank that her brain was wasting away, along with her body.

"Not much of a life, this," Eliza said.

Hank felt ashamed, as if she had read his mind. He tried to respond, but could not find the words.

"Maybe I should call that guy..."

Hank waited, wanting to help, but at a loss. He cocked his head.

Rocking gently in the chair, she scrunched her face, searching for the name of "that guy." After a long moment, her eyebrows shot up. "Doctor Death."

"Ah." Hank nodded. "Jack Kevorkian." The man who'd been performing physician-assisted suicides for the sick and elderly.

"That's him!"

"Sorry, dear, they sent him to prison for murder."

Eliza shook her head. "Imagine that. We live in a strange world, don't we?"

Hank nodded while his pulse quickened.

"And now we've got this other case..."

This time, Hank knew immediately what she was referring to. "Terri Schiavo." It had been a top news story for a while.

"Yes." Eliza narrowed her eyes. "That poor woman's a vegetable. I'm with her husband on this one."

Hank chewed the inside of his cheek, eyes averted. With his own circumstances gnawing at him like a ravenous hog, he too could sympathize with the husband, although it seemed plenty of people were not so inclined. He started to open his mouth, but something inside him fought off the temptation, stifling the question in his throat.

When he eventually turned back to Eliza, her gaze was fixed across the room. Hank followed her line of sight to Brenda's desk. Brenda's *shrine* was more like it because Eliza had not changed a thing since their daughter's death.

The framed photo of mother and daughter occupied one corner. Brenda, smiling radiantly, captured for eternity in the prime of her youth. It was as though her enduring memory would be forever shielded from the ravages of old age—the very ravages now overtaking Eliza.

Tacked on the wall behind the photo, an array of four equestrian competition ribbons: blue, red, green, and white. On the opposite side of the desk, a stack of three books: *Of Mice and Men* and *Lord of the Flies,* which had been school reading assignments, underneath *Rosemary's Baby,* her entertainment reading. Brenda had always been an avid reader, and she loved the macabre. Behind the books, her lava lamp, unlit for thirty years, stood sentry in the corner.

"Death..." Eliza's voice punctured the silence of the room. "...it's just another part of life."

When Hank turned back to face Eliza, she leveled her gaze at him. "It's my time, Hank."

As her words simmered, Hank felt a sting in his eyes, but he blinked it away. He swallowed, then started to open his mouth once again, but the same inner force suppressed it.

"I've had a good life." She halted for a gulp of air. "And I'm not afraid to die."

Hank swallowed while Eliza took another breath. She cleared her throat before adding, "I'm more worried about you than me, dear."

Unsure of what she meant, Hank tilted his head, knitting his brow.

"You're the one who's going to have to adjust."

He considered this. Perhaps it was true, although he had not given it any thought. Eliza *was* the last of his family. What would life be like without her? Except, now wasn't the time to think about that. "You don't need to worry about me."

Studying him with piercing eyes and a wrinkled nose, Eliza nodded slowly. "Anyway, maybe I'll see Brenda."

Hank gave a frail smile while a suffocating hush spread through the room.

A minute or so later, a barn owl's screech cut through the night, sending a chill through Hank's bones.

"That's our cue." Eliza pulled herself up from the rocking chair before Hank could position himself to help her. "It's night-night time."

He shuffled clear of the bed. "Want the window closed?"

"Yeah, the nights are getting chilly."

They had already placed her favorite quilt on the bed, which had been in summer exile. Eliza had made it for Brenda when she was a toddler and always referred to it as the "pink quilt." Since the beginning, Hank wondered what made it "pink." It was *many* colors—it was a quilt, after all. He eventually decided if he stared at it long enough in an unfocused way, pink was as prominent of a color as any other.

As Eliza slid under the covers, Hank pushed down the sash and drew the curtains together. "Need anything else?" he asked as he bent to kiss her goodnight.

"No thanks," she said, tilting her head back onto the pillow. "Good night, dear."

Outside, somewhere in the distance, the owl shrieked once again.

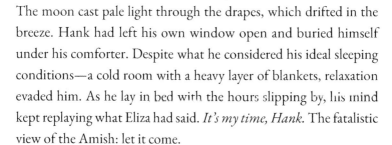

The moon cast pale light through the drapes, which drifted in the breeze. Hank had left his own window open and buried himself under his comforter. Despite what he considered his ideal sleeping conditions—a cold room with a heavy layer of blankets, relaxation evaded him. As he lay in bed with the hours slipping by, his mind kept replaying what Eliza had said. *It's my time, Hank.* The fatalistic view of the Amish: let it come.

But letting it come...that's different from making it happen, *right?*

Eliza had said, "Death is part of life."

But if you know death is imminent, and living merely means suffering, what's wrong with getting there sooner?

Doctor Death.

Jack Kevorkian had plenty to say on the matter.

The poor fellow is in prison, though, Hank thought. Society had roundly rejected the advocate of physician-assisted suicide. Then again, maybe part of the problem was he was so vocal and public in his actions. He might have been better off acting as a silent practitioner than an evangelist.

Although Eliza would never have complained, it was clear her suffering was becoming intolerable. At first, it was just headaches, dizziness, and forgetfulness. Then came "psychotic" episodes and seizures, which were becoming more frequent with each passing week. What would be next?

And then there was the breathing. Initially, shortness of breath and wheezing. Later, what they call "air hunger." Next, "air starvation" seemed inevitable. Hank sighed and rolled onto his back, gluing his gaze to the ceiling, shimmering under the shifting moonlight.

Air starvation. What a horrible feeling: like drowning, but without any water.

It seemed clear that much of society wanted the preservation of life...at *any* cost. Except, what sort of husband would he be if he just let Eliza's suffering continue—if he just stood by, doing nothing, while it worsened? Where was the mercy in that?

Yet mercy was within his reach. He'd even given a name to it: "The Deed."

The Devil's work, Reverend Burns had called the idea. In hindsight, Hank's confession—and any expectation of support and understanding from the so-called "spiritual leader"—was folly. *What the heck were you thinking, Old Man?* The pastor adhered to rigid morality guidelines. Regardless, did Hank really need someone else to tell him what was wrong and what was right?

Eliza needed him, that much was clear. He had spent the past couple of months feeling helpless. The Deed offered him a way to take action. He could bring an end to her suffering.

Earlier, he had almost gone as far as to ask Eliza if she wanted him to end it. But he'd held back. What if she said no? Would he then have to stand by and watch her endure in misery? Putting the question to her seemed like shirking the burden of his decision, and that would have been unfair to Eliza. Besides, she had all but told him it was okay, had she not?

As Hank began drifting off to sleep, he felt at peace with what he needed to do, and conviction gelled in his mind. The only real question was when? Waiting too long meant more suffering. And it was not hard to imagine an episode leading to some horrible outcome. As the days passed, Eliza was in an increasingly precarious position: one seizure-invoked fall away from a broken hip or neck—on Hank's watch, no less. On the other hand, performing The Deed too soon meant they'd miss out on their last remaining good moments together. Would he know when it was time to carry through with his plans?

These questions dissolved away as he dipped into slumber.

The barn owl screeched, jarring Hank awake, but as he clawed his way back into consciousness, he found himself overwhelmed with guilt. *How could I even consider such a thing?*

CHAPTER 10

———◇———

AUTUMN

SEPTEMBER 30, 2002

H ANK PLACED THE SMALL oxygen tank in the middle of the pickup's bench seat and then helped Eliza up from the wheelchair and into the cab.

"Did you bring your magazine?"

Still recovering from the effort, Eliza formed an "o" with her lips and looked around.

Hank rummaged in the back pocket of the wheelchair, and there it was. He smiled and handed her the *Reader's Digest.*

"Thank you, dear. Except I'm not sure why I even bother anymore. I can't make much sense out of the articles these days."

"Maybe it's good exercise for the brain," Hank said while buckling her in, although he doubted it really worked that way.

He collapsed the wheelchair and lifted it into the truck bed. Taking the wheelchair along was merely a precaution; since she could no longer be left at home alone, their plan was for Eliza to remain in the truck while he ran errands. It was not a risk-free strategy, but it was better than the alternatives.

He backed down the drive, turning into the gravel roadway, and they set off for Clarkton. The pickup rolled past the ruins of Shirley

Gould's house, and just beyond, rounded the bend in the road where the grade sloped upward.

"Oh, my," Eliza said, looking ahead. Vibrant colors slashed through the woodland patches enclosing the roadway. "Fall is here."

"Our favorite time of the year," Hank said. "It'll be peak color soon."

"And you just can't beat this weather."

Hank nodded. Early autumn was often as good as Ohio weather offered: warm days with low humidity, cool nights, and long stretches with seldom a passing stray cloud in the sky. It was a welcome break from the "dog days" of summer.

"Autumn's too short," Eliza said.

"Ain't that the truth?" It was a cruel irony: the glorious color carried a melancholy sentiment that fall would pass quickly. Over the next six weeks, the fiery burgundies, reds, and oranges would be first crowded out by yellows, which would then leach away, leaving behind gloomy shades of brown and gray. The dead of winter would progressively tighten its grip, squeezing life from the land.

"We'll enjoy it while it lasts." Eliza gazed out the window as if soaking it all in.

When the pickup crested the hill, the road suddenly filled with an oncoming semi-truck. Eliza flinched and let out a yelp as she braced herself.

Hank slammed on the brakes, skidding the pickup on the gravel. The semi did the same, and both vehicles came to a nose-to-nose stop within a dense cloud of road dust.

Blowing out an exasperated breath, Hank pressed his head back against the headrest, waiting for the air to clear, while telling himself to keep his cool.

Without speaking, Eliza picked up the mask and pressed it against her face. Hank opened the valve for her, noting the gauge read almost empty. One of his tasks for the outing would be replacing the tank.

As visibility improved, the truck's door swung open. Hank put the gearshift in park and climbed out.

The truck driver's hanging belly jiggled as he tromped down the ladder with considerable effort. "Man, that was close!"

"I'll say," Hank said as he squeezed through the narrow gap between the two bumpers. Tempted to go off on the trucker, he thought better of it, knowing it was best to avoid risking a fight he had little hope of winning. "You were going too fast for this road."

"Sorry, man. Never expected to run into anyone else on this Po-dunk road."

Although Hank's blood was boiling over because of how close he and Eliza had come to being flattened, he had to admit there was truth in the man's words. Rarely did two vehicles cross paths on the single-lane township road. Nonetheless, it obviously did happen on occasion.

Peering along the side of the road, Hank examined the truck's contents: an immense stack of cinder block. "You dropping that off down yonder?"

"You got it." The fat man scanned the roadway behind Hank. "Is there a pullout nearby?"

Hank knew where each of the dozen or so pullouts were located along the country road's length. "Of course, you just passed the closest one."

The truck driver turned back and looked in the direction from which he'd come. "Flippin' figures."

"It wouldn't be easy for you to back that rig up, so I'll reverse down the hill."

"Much obliged," the trucker said with a head nod, and both men returned to their vehicles.

As Hank slid behind the wheel, Eliza took off the mask and closed the valve. "Where's he going with that load?" she asked.

Hank hesitated, putting on a show of concentration as he backed down the slope. Halfway there, he ran out of time. "It's block, for the foundations of the new houses," he said in a casual way, downplaying the impending new neighbors. Although Hank had not spoken to Levi Hostetler since that day when the Amishman had stopped to introduce himself, Hank had waved to the men as he'd seen them coming and going. When he and Eliza had driven through the back way the weekend prior, the plot of land—and the remains of Hillbilly Cabin—had pretty much already been cleared.

"The new Amish homes?" Eliza asked with a rattle in her breath.

Hank nodded as he nudged into the turnout. Unsure of what he could say to keep her from getting riled up on the matter, he left it at that.

The semi crept down the hill and the trucker waved "thanks" as he rumbled by.

"Are you still up for going?" Hank asked.

Eliza nodded. When she saw his *are-you-sure* questioning look, she added, "Let's go."

He coaxed the pickup back onto the roadway and ascended the hill one more time.

They passed two other abandoned houses as they proceeded along the country road. Shirley Gould's former home (commonly known as Ghoul House these days) was just one of a dozen dotting the four-and-a-half-mile stretch through the Salem Valley. When Hank was a child, there had been quite a few more active households along the township road. Through the generations, much of the soil lost its fertility because of poor farming practices. Properties were deserted as families departed seeking better prospects, and the fields left behind had gone fallow.

The derelict homes stood in defiance of time, their wood siding bleached into a sickly dull gray by the endless cycles of harsh winters and blazing summer sunlight. Windows and doors had long since been busted from their frames, leaving gaping holes that made the structures appear like cast-off skulls—empty eye sockets devoid of life, jaws cocked open in an eternal, silent scream. Floors sagged and roofs gradually collapsed. The hollowed-out buildings were left to decay while the woods grew closer each season, surrounding and consuming them.

The gravel road ended at the state route, a winding two-lane high-way leading into Clarkton. Hank maneuvered through the junction's turnoff to retrieve their mail, pulling up to their postal box beside two others. The other resident families on the township road had their boxes at the opposite end, which was closer to them.

"It's crammed full," Hank said when he opened the box. He began fishing portions of the jammed pile out, handing them to Eliza in bunches.

"We used to collect it three times a week," Eliza said.

"Let it wait." Hank laughed. "Nowadays, it's just bills and junk mail."

Eliza shuffled absently through the mail multiple times as they drove.

Twenty minutes later, they came upon Hank's favorite produce stand, a few miles before the rural scenery transitioned into the southern end of Clarkton's commercial district. "We're overdue for our pumpkins," he said as he pulled the truck in, parking in front of the small building.

Eliza smiled, put the pile of mail down, and opened the *Reader's Digest*.

For Hank and Eliza, growing their own produce had always been a point of pride, but by the time they approached seventy, they had lost their motivation for the backbreaking work. Over the past five years, they'd been buying their produce from local stands—and in Eliza's judgment, *this* one offered the best baked goods.

The first thing Hank did was head over to the rows of pumpkins, arranged by size, with a wooden stake pounded into the ground in front of each line, indicating the price for that batch.

The Amish did not carve pumpkins into jack-o'-lanterns or otherwise recognize Halloween, because of its pagan origins and the not uncommon but misguided belief that the holiday was a "celebration of the Devil." So, Hank always found it a bit funny how many of them had no compunction growing pumpkins to sell to the "English" for that very purpose.

He looked the first row over, searching for one with an unusual shape, a tradition Brenda had started when she was young. She would always hunt for the ugly ones—the pickings nobody else would want. Hank had stopped carving pumpkins after Brenda passed away, but he still made a point of buying a couple each year to set on the porch steps, and, knowing how much she'd approve, he'd still search for the oddball ones.

He spotted a tall, thin one sitting behind a stake with PUMKINS $3 written on it. With a grin at the misspelled word, he retrieved his selection and set it aside. He moved on to the PUMKINS $2 row and found one with an odd narrowing in the middle, an unusual shape that reminded him of a skull. After relocating it next to his skinny choice, he scanned the rest of the lot, finding a perfectly symmetrical, short, and wide specimen, which soon joined the others.

Eliza watched him with a distant look in her eyes.

"I'm splurging. Getting three this year," he said with a grin before turning toward the building. *Brenda would be proud,* he silently asserted, but decided against saying it out loud.

He passed a large wooden box bolted to the side of the building beside the door, with a narrow slot cut in the top and a small padlock dangling from the front. Underneath the lock, words were scrawled in marker:

SELF SERVE WHEN CLOSED
NO SUNDAY SALES
THANK YOU

The Amish stands always made such a point of specifying "No Sunday Sales," which made Hank wonder what an Amishman would do if he discovered on Monday morning that someone had left cash in his self-serve box the day prior. *I'm doomed! I made a Sunday sale!* He smiled at the thought and reached for the door.

When he stepped inside, Hank pulled off his hat and hello-nodded to Nettie, the young Amish woman arranging vegetables in the bins. She responded with a curt, "Good morning," without stopping what she was doing.

Hank had seen Nettie working her family's stand since he started frequenting the place, although he couldn't remember how he'd learned her name. Regardless, she expressed no indication of familiarity to him on this occasion, or any previous visit, for that matter. *Hopefully, she's friendlier with her own kind.* Hank had his doubts though, considering she was not yet married and was probably on the verge of becoming a spinster for life.

He approached the wooden crate with a handwritten note card hanging on the side: MUSKMELLON 50¢ EA. Melon was misspelled with two Ls, but Hank always cut the Amish plenty of slack when it came to grammar errors. They used Old Dutch as their first language, only using English when communicating with "the English." Cantaloupes were called "muskmelon" by the Amish. He assumed the name came from the odor they gave off as they ripened, which he supposed *could* be described as musky. After looking through the lot, he picked out the largest he could find, then felt along its surface to confirm it had no bruises.

A zucchini, cabbage, green pepper, and cucumber, plus two acorn squashes and three tomatoes later, Hank moved on to peruse the baked goods, arranged on shelving near the cash register. He picked a loaf of zucchini bread and a peach fry pie, both Eliza's favorites, placing them on the counter beside his selection of produce. Then he returned to the shelf and grabbed a jar of homemade apple butter. "I also got seven dollars' worth of pumpkins."

Nettie fished a short pencil out of the tiny pocket sewn into the side of her long blue dress. While she went about tallying the items in a spiral notebook, Hank examined the hand-scrawled paper sign tacked on the wall behind the counter:

LAST DAY OF THE SEASON
SATURDAY OCTOBER 5

The shuttered produce stands were a sad annual harbinger of the looming end of nice weather, and a sure indication that winter would soon be upon them.

He wandered over to the window to check on Eliza, who was thumbing through the magazine. As silly as it sounded, Hank was enjoying the produce stand visit, feeling like it was a little outing, all within watchful eyeshot of his ailing wife. With little in the way of time to himself these days, he missed his alone time—especially his fishing diversions, which were now out of the question.

"That'll be nineteen dollars and seventy-five cents."

Hank returned to the counter as Nettie slipped the pencil back into her pocket and started bagging the goods.

"You're closing this weekend," Hank said, pointing with his chin at the sign on the wall.

"Not much growing anymore, besides pumpkin and squash," Nettie spoke without ever looking up. "We're selling those, self-serve, until the end of October."

"It's a shame fall is so short," Hank said. "Winter seems so long. It gets depressing." All of a sudden, he thought forward to the coming season, filling him with dread. By Thanksgiving, daily frost would form on the ground. By Christmas, chilling winds whistling through the bare trees would bring snow. As winter settled in, smothering the countryside in icy darkness, the remote privacy of the farm would descend first into solitary isolation, then desolate despair.

Just him...alone.

When he pulled himself back into the moment, Hank found Nettie looking him in the eye, catching him off guard. Was this the first time she'd ever made eye contact?

"Winter is God's way of cleaning house." She spoke steadily, her gaze fixed on him so intently that he felt like she was peering *into* him. "The weak trees, weak animals...the weak won't make it. But that makes room for younger and stronger ones in the spring."

Unable to respond, Hank simply nodded in silence.

Nettie held her stare for a spell before abruptly breaking eye contact and returning to the task of bagging his produce.

Slow to recover from the thunderstrike, Hank urged himself to quit standing there like a scarecrow and do something, then remembered he needed to pay. He pulled his wallet out and fumbled through it for a twenty-dollar bill.

"Thank you," she said when he handed the cash to her. She removed a quarter from the cash box, and when she handed it to him, she locked eyes with him once again and smiled.

Until that exchange, Hank was pretty sure he'd never seen the young woman smile. It made him feel so unsettled he almost wished she hadn't. He gathered the bags, and as he turned away from the counter, her words echoed in his mind: *Winter is God's way of cleaning house. The weak don't make it.*

As he pushed open the door, he forced himself to say, "Take care."

"See you again in the spring..." she called after him as he stepped outside.

Hank blinked in the sunlight, wondering, *Was that a question?* There had been a slight upward inflection on the final word, hadn't there?

Eliza leaned out the window, looking his way. "Everything okay, dear?" she asked, breaking him free from his stupor.

Hank nodded, feeling sheepish because she was asking him; it was him who should have been checking on her. Walking over to the passenger door, he put his haul down on the gravel. He hunted through the bags and withdrew the zucchini bread, holding the loaf out like an offering. Eliza took it and laid it on her lap without providing the enthusiastic reaction he expected.

After packing the bags in the bed's cargo storage net, Hank arranged the pumpkins in the corner, tucked behind the wheelchair, which he bungee-corded in place. Hopefully, he would remember to drive gently, so the pumpkins would stay put. Before closing the liftgate, he located the fry pie, which he carried into the cab.

Behind the wheel, Hank showed her the pie and then began unwrapping it. "We'll split this. It's peach."

Eliza wrinkled her nose. "I'm not really hungry."

Hank studied her, but she offered no further explanation. He wrapped the pie back up and placed it in the console. "We'll save it for later, then."

After putting on his seatbelt, he started the truck and shifted into reverse.

As he backed away from the produce stand, Eliza let out a gasp, startling Hank. He froze, and when he followed where her eyes were aiming, he saw Nettie peering at them through the dusty windowpane of the produce stand. Her disembodied face seemed to float unnaturally in the darkness beyond, the light filtering through the cloudy glass, casting strange shadows on her features. Hank shuddered.

The young woman stepped back from the window, and in an instant, her face was gone, leaving only blackness in its place.

CHAPTER 11

LAST DAYS

OCTOBER 7, 2002

H ANK HELD ONTO ONE of the thicker tree branches to help him balance on the ladder. He reached out with his free hand, plucked an apple, and looked it over. It had a perfect red color all the way around, but most importantly, no worm blemishes. He placed it with the others in the canvas bag hanging from his waist and looked the lot over. Considering their relatively small size, he would need to collect at least ten for a decent batch of applesauce. Almost there.

Hank rested before going for another, savoring the crisp early fall day from his perch on the ladder. The smell of autumn hung in the air, and bright colors engulfed the full span of foliage surrounding the farmhouse. Although most of the leaves remained on the trees, some were beginning to drop, churning and darting in the breeze as they fell to the ground.

He reached out and grabbed the next branch, leaning on it gently as his weight shifted forward. Suddenly, the limb gave way with a snap, and Hank felt himself falling forward. In a flash of panic, he flailed for the top ladder rung with his free hand, catching hold of it just in time. He reestablished his balance and pushed himself upright. *Geez,* he thought, staring down at the ground he had almost tumbled to. The drop of twelve feet or more would have been ugly.

As he took in a series of calming breaths, he looked over at Eliza, in her wheelchair on the front porch. She gazed off into the distance, oblivious to his near catastrophe.

What if he *had* fallen? Eliza would not have been able to help him. Worse yet, who would care for her if something bad happened to him? Hank shuddered at the unanswerable question.

He peeked into the bag, gauging whether he'd collected enough. Maybe so. Nonetheless, he spotted an extra plump specimen within easy enough reach when he looked up. Stretching carefully for a solid-looking branch, he tested it, then used his other hand to grab hold of the apple.

"Uhhhhh..."

Hank recognized the sound immediately as Eliza's seizure-onset moan. But he was in too precarious of a position to even look her way. He twisted the apple free, dropped it in the bag, and then secured a grip on the ladder before releasing the branch. With both hands stabilizing him, he turned back for a glance. Her body had gone rigid, her head tilted back and up.

Before stepping down, Hank hesitated for just a wink while a thought crossed his mind: *Should I leave her be?* The question flitted into his conscience without warning, and he immediately swatted it away, appalled. *Did I really think that?* he wondered as he scaled down to the ground, knocking his cap off along the way.

He rushed across the lawn and leaped up the steps, sending several apples tumbling from the bag and rolling across the porch floor. The doctor had stressed how important it was for Eliza to have oxygen during a seizure, so he grabbed the mask and pressed it against her blue-tinged face as he opened the valve.

She twitched. A thin band of white was exposed between not-quite-closed eyelids. Hank found himself wondering what Eliza felt during a seizure. Does she experience anything at all? Or would it be like dying in her sleep? Her arms and legs tensed, then relaxed, repeating over several cycles, slower each time.

Oh, poor Eliza, Hank thought while the seconds ticked by. *Am I waiting too long to do The Deed?*

As her body slackened, her eyes began rolling back into their normal position. She pushed open her eyelids and blinked twice before dropping into a deep sleep.

———◆———

Hank stirred the applesauce mindlessly, his brain fixated on that nasty fleeting thought.

Should I leave her be?

How could he have asked this? That would be the coward's path, and there was no mercy in that, was there? Even if it had come from the depths of his subconscious, the shameful notion was his own, and he felt dirty from it.

Honking geese pulled him back into the here and now. He peered out the window in time to see a couple of dozen birds flying south across the valley in a V-formation.

"That's our first sighting of migrating geese this season," he said to Eliza, parked in her wheelchair behind him, at the kitchen table.

She lifted her head and considered what he said for a spell before responding, "It's almost spring."

Hank opened his mouth to correct her, then snapped it shut. With his throat tightening, he turned away to face the sink. He focused on the knickknacks lined up on the windowsill above the faucet. A brass donkey bottle opener, its mouth serving as the lever for the cap. A paperweight fashioned from polished agate. A ceramic lighthouse, the detachable upper level a salt shaker, the lower level, pepper. All items his mother had placed there eons ago.

Taking notice of a thick layer of dust blanketing the sill, Hank ran his fingertip through it, exposing a trail of smooth, white painted surface. *Eliza wouldn't have let this happen,* he pointed out to himself as he rubbed his fingertips together to clear the residue off. Although he had no problem taking over the household duties, the transition had been tough on her. Nonetheless, she had stayed out of his new business. She had no way of changing the circumstances, so she allowed him to find his way.

He picked the big wooden spoon back up and stirred the applesauce one more time. After swallowing to clear what felt like a horse pill lodged in his throat, he took a taste, making a show of the act for Eliza. "Mmmm."

She gave a weak smile.

He turned off the burner and carried a spoonful to her. She tasted it and licked her lips, nodding slowly, wearing a worn-out expression on her face. It had been several hours since the seizure, but the effects lingered. Perhaps the attack even took a lasting toll. It seemed to Hank that each episode had nibbled away a little more of her spirit.

When he looked at the clock, Hank was surprised to see it was almost suppertime already. "Are you okay with TV dinners again tonight?"

"Of course, dear," Eliza said in a gravelly wheeze. She lifted the mask to her face.

Hank opened the valve for her. "We'll have fresh applesauce as a side dish. Heck, we'll be eating that for the next week or two."

After spooning out their two bowls of applesauce, he covered the pot with its aluminum lid and took it down to the cellar. Just as Ma had always done, he placed the pot on the dirt floor beside the steps to let it cool, cocking the lid a sliver so the heat could escape.

Upon his return to the kitchen, Eliza removed the mask. He shut the valve, then went searching through the freezer for her favorite TV dinner. Locating one, he held up the package. She stared at it with a blank expression. "What is it?" she asked, as if somehow, she could no longer read. Even the photo on the package seemed to sweep past her without registering.

"Chicken Fried Steak with Gravy."

She nodded faintly, with a far-off expression.

Hank picked a Meatloaf supper for himself, then set the oven to preheat. "It'll be forty-five minutes before these are ready, dear. How does a nap sound?"

Eliza shrugged, but her head bobbed approval.

After releasing the brake, he wheeled her past the dining room and into the parlor, where he helped her into the daybed. She closed her eyes. He bent over and kissed her head. She gave no reaction, but her breaths deepened.

When Hank turned away from the daybed, movement outside caught his attention. He stepped up to the window and watched two buggies passing the farmhouse, the Amishmen done working for the day.

Early that morning, for the first time since they had met, Hank had spoken with Levi Hostetler, when the men came through on their way to the worksite. The soon-to-be Amish neighbors were constructing cinder-block foundations for the three homes. Levi reported that carpentry would begin in another week. When that happened, the site would be swarmed by every male member of their community at least thirteen years of age. *Like a barn-raising,* Hank figured. *More like a triple house-raising.* Levi estimated they would complete the task in less than two weeks. Throughout its life, Township Road 223 had rarely seen the type of traffic it would soon see.

Eliza snorted. He turned around and silently watched over her as she settled into a rattling snore. An odd question formed in Hank's head: would his wife even be around long enough to help him finish that batch of applesauce?

CHAPTER 12

---◆○◆---

THE DEED

OCTOBER 14, 2002

H ANK MITCHELL WOKE UP to the sound of Eliza coughing from her bedroom. He waited, listening, trying to judge whether she needed help, but she soon tapered off.

Predawn light had infiltrated the night sky. The clock on his nightstand read 7:25. Soon, the sun would rise. As he stretched in bed, the curtain drifted in, carried on a mild breeze. They were in the midst of a string of unseasonably warm and dry days, which Ma and Pop referred to as "Indian summer" when such a pattern occurred this late in the year.

Hank slipped out of bed and, making a point of treading on the uncreaky portions of the floor, set about changing from his pajamas into clothes. A new noise caught his attention, and he stopped to listen. Outside. Popping gravel. He peered through the gap in the curtains and nodded when he spotted an Amish buggy rolling along the road, followed by three others in the distance. *The triple house raising begins.* More would surely follow.

He watched as the buggies passed. Peak fall color had erupted through the surrounding landscape, providing a vibrant panorama, even in the feeble early morning light.

A sudden crash resounded from down the hall. "What the devil?" he muttered under his breath as he stumbled across the room and into the corridor. His heart thrummed as he approached Eliza's room. When he stepped into the doorway, he found her face-down on the floor, bound in the bedsheet and pink quilt, her body clenched in a seizure. Lurching forward, he dropped to his knees at her side, ignoring the warm puddle soaking through the fabric of his pants. "Oh, Eliza..."

He reached for the oxygen tank, which lay on its side, beside the toppled nightstand. She had knocked over both when she tumbled out of bed. After rotating the valve open, he traced the rubber hose in search of the mask buried underneath her. He rolled over her stiff and twitching body, sweeping the plastic cup out from under her at the sight of it.

As he prepared to bring the mask to her face, he paused for an instant to look her over. Bright red blood was smeared around her lips, a garish contrast to the blue color of her face. An angry purple bruise had already started forming on her swelling cheekbone, apparently from a bump she had sustained in the fall.

Hank held the mask over her ghastly red lips with a quivering hand and counted the passing seconds. The familiar sight of her eye whites peeked through the gap between her lids. Her limbs convulsed under the quilt, but before long, her body started going limp. She blinked several times, then her eyelids closed, and she began to snore.

"I've waited too long," he murmured as a seed of clarity took root in his mind.

Squeezing his free palm against his forehead, he questioned whether he should try to lift her into the bed, but decided it was more important to keep the oxygen mask on her face. As he waited, he looked around. When he noticed a bloody handkerchief that had fallen to the floor when the nightstand had toppled, the blood smears on her lips suddenly made sense. *She was coughing up blood,* he realized with dismay.

Hank moaned, sniffed, then whispered, "I'm so sorry, dear."

<hr />

When Eliza came to, Hank removed the mask from her face and gave her the best smile he could manage. Her eyes volleyed about her surroundings as she brought her fingers up to her swollen cheek-bone, patting it gingerly. She gave two brisk wet coughs, sputtering red droplets on the back of Hank's hands. "What happened?" she croaked.

"You fell out of bed," he said in a no-big-deal tone. "Let me help you up."

Without waiting for a response, he slid his arms underneath her and lifted her off the floor. Despite recognizing her state of atrophy, he was still surprised at how light she had become.

He laid her on the mattress and straightened her bed covers and pillow. Her eyelids sank, perhaps weighed down more by weariness rather than a sense of comfort, and while Hank went about righting the nightstand and rearranging the items that had been knocked to the floor, Eliza fell back asleep.

What Hank Mitchell did next, he did with remarkably little hesitation or emotion. While the conviction filling his mind left little room for second thoughts, he knew certitude might wane if he did not act decisively. *Don't dawdle, Old Man. You've put this off long enough.*

After his morning pee, face rinse, and teeth brushing, Hank studied his reflection in the mirror. An aging man stared back at him, but he could discern no sign of weakness or doubt. He checked on Eliza, who remained sound asleep, then dried her legs and mopped the floor with a towel before heading downstairs.

Back in the kitchen, he measured out four tablespoons of coffee grounds from the red Folgers can, dumping them into a paper filter. He filled the reservoir to the well water's crusty mineral residue line and slid the switch to BREW. The coffeemaker gurgled as he walked out the back door and into the subtle morning warmth.

Crossing the yard, he paused beside the well, placing his palms over the grindstone cap. Brenda and Eliza both had loved the quaint wooden wishing well structure that once occupied this spot, accompanied by a winch for raising and lowering the water bucket, covered with a traditional wooden roof. When electricity came to the Salem Valley in 1948, Pop electrified the farmhouse, adding an electric pump for the well water, rendering the bucket and its crank ornamental. Over the years, Hank patched the wooden structure as sections rotted. But eventually, it had decayed beyond repair, so in the 1980s he removed it and simply capped the well with an old grindstone, its center hole plugged with a locust tree branch. Brenda was gone by then. Knowing it was not practical to rebuild the original structure, Eliza never complained, but Hank knew how much she hated losing it.

First, Brenda had departed. Then, the wishing well. Next, Eliza.

With a lump forming in his throat, Hank swallowed, turned away from the well, and regarded his surroundings. Birds sang in the branches of the buckeye tree above him, and rays of sunshine projected from beyond the eastern stretch of woods, brightening their glorious blend of colors. It struck Hank as wrong that he would perform The Deed on such a beautiful morning. The *Dirty* Deed. *No qualms*, he reminded himself, setting off across the grass.

As he approached the barn, the sound of horses clopping arose in the distance. He hurriedly opened the barn's man door and tucked into the shadows, watching as three more buggies rolled in the direction of the Mitchell farmhouse, passing Shirley Gould's home.

Hank pushed the door almost closed, leaving enough of a gap to let in a wedge of sunlight. Withdrawing into the musty interior, the path darkened as he trekked back toward the workbench. His footfalls on the densely packed dirt floor echoed through the barn, spooking a feral tomcat that had snuck in through one of the many voids in the siding. With a hiss, it scurried away into the gloom.

The upper-level window on the eastern side projected a bright shaft of morning light, emblazing a galaxy of swirling dust that Hank ventured into. The visual effect only added to the surreal feeling sloshing around in his head.

Once in the workshop, he switched on the overhead lights, spotlighting an expansive spiderweb that stretched from the pegboard behind the workbench to the vise on the front corner. A wicked-looking spider scooted along the web and withdrew into a pocket near the vise.

Hank had always been more squeamish about spiders than any self-respecting farmer should ever be, but at this moment his preoccupied brain hardly noticed. He reached around the web and popped open the rusty metal cabinet housing the long-dormant horse care supplies.

A vial, cloaked in a thick layer of dust, stood sentry in the bottom corner. He plucked it from the shelf and studied it. Xylazine. Horse tranquilizer, left behind by the veterinarian in the days when Eliza kept her equines. Doctor Votram had warned them about the toxicity of the drug to humans, recounting how one of her vet school classmates had committed suicide by ingesting it. He palmed the small bottle, swung the cabinet closed, and snapped off the workbench lights before heading back to the house.

When Hank entered the kitchen, the coffeemaker gave its final extra-long gurgle, then belched a puff of steam, signaling the completion of the brew cycle.

As the coffee finished dripping, he placed two slices of bread in the toaster, noticing the specks of dried blood Eliza had coughed onto the backs of his hands. He did not bother to wash them off.

Pouring coffee into Eliza's mug, he studied the remaining traces of its **Homer County Fair 1978** emblem. She had received the cup and a blue ribbon in the equestrian competition that year, the first exhibition she had competed in after Brenda's death. Although the mug's emblem was barely visible after twenty-four years of daily use, she still cherished this possession as a token of her strength, a small triumph over six years of depression.

He added a shot of milk to her coffee and stirred it slowly, eyeing the vial of xylazine sitting nearby. *Don't back out now,* some distant voice in his head implored. *You've waited too long already.*

He tore off a paper towel, dampened it, then picked up the bottle and wiped the dust off. Half full...but how much to use? It was a horse tranquilizer, so a fraction of the vial should be plenty. Maybe ten percent?

After pulling off the rubber stopper, he sniffed the contents. The drug had no smell. He tipped the bottle over the mug, trickling some into the coffee. He hesitated, then splashed in more before checking the level, judging that he had used about a third of what was there. With a nod, he reinserted the stopper and tucked the vial behind the sugar canister and against the wall.

The toaster popped, causing Hank to flinch. He buried his face in his hands and sighed. *Keep it together, Old Man.* The numbness he felt earlier had flagged; his mind now buzzed with nervous tension.

Drawing in a sharp breath, he stirred Eliza's coffee one more time, then filled his John Deere mug and spread apple butter over the toast. He arranged the cups, the plate of toast, and two napkins on a wooden tray. Within seconds of lifting the tray, the ceramics were chattering against each other. Hank tried to steady his hands while he headed to the front of the house.

At the foot of the stairway, he sidestepped the wheelchair and paused, gazing up at the empty hallway. He listened, but he heard nothing through the throbbing sensation in his head. Although he ascended on tiptoes, his feet grew heavier with each step, becoming chunks of granite near the top. He held up there, the tray trembling in his grasp, then dragged himself onward, toward the far end of the hall.

When he peeked into her bedroom, Eliza was awake, patting her swollen cheek, her eyes shimmering in discomfort. "G'morning," he said, trying to use a chipper tone while carrying the tray over to the dresser.

"Good morning." Eliza gave a tepid smile and dabbed her bruise with one finger. "I don't know why, but my cheek hurts."

With a galloping heart, Hank leaned over her and pretended to examine the bright purple spot. "Hmmm. But it doesn't look bad. Maybe having coffee and toast in bed will help." He reached across the bed for the other pillow, helped her sit upright, and then propped her against a makeshift pillow lounge.

"Thanks, dear." Eliza voiced the words with a wet sputter.

"Do you need oxygen?"

She shook her head.

He brought the tray over, swung down the legs, and placed it over her lap. She immediately picked up her prized mug and took a sip of the coffee.

As Hank pulled the rocking chair up next to the bed, he monitored Eliza's face for any unusual reaction but discerned none. He took the John Deere mug from the tray, then lowered himself into the chair, watching while she took another sip. She picked up the toast, nibbled a corner, and placed it back on the plate.

Hank concentrated on trying to look calm. Despite the lump blocking his throat, he sipped his coffee, rocking slightly in the chair, just enough to cause the familiar creak in the floorboards with each roll.

Eliza coughed into her napkin, turning a splotch of it red. She reclined against the pillows, giving no indication she noticed. "Have you been up long?"

The floor creaked with his backward rock. "No, not long." Hank blinked to suppress the sting in his eyes and took another drink.

While Eliza sat motionless, the floorboard creaked three more times.

In a snap, a horrible thought presented itself to Hank: What if she drank enough to hurt her, but not kill? He imagined having to rush her to the hospital. *Oh, God...*

Just as this concern began to escalate into a full-blown panic, Eliza broke out of her daze and picked the mug up. She made a slurping sound as she took a long sip.

When she placed the drink back down, it was a quarter gone.

A small part of Hank began questioning whether he was doing the right thing. If not, was it too late to stop her, or had she already consumed too much of the drug? His gaze shifted down to his lap.

When his sight focused on the dried blood specks on his hands, the second-guessing thoughts dispersed.

"It looks like a nice day," Eliza said in a weak voice, peering at the window. "I wish I could go for a walk."

In the most collected demeanor he could muster, Hank nodded and took in a gulp of his coffee. "It's Indian summer."

Eliza's breath rasped unevenly. The clock ticked behind him, and Hank found himself synchronizing the floorboard creaks to every fourth second.

Please drink more, he pleaded inside his mind, guessing that she needed to at least drink half.

As if in response, Eliza picked up the coffee mug and took another swallow, followed it with a nibble of toast, then one more swig. When she put the cup back down, it was half gone. "Indian summer," she muttered, her words slurring, and whatever thought she had seemed to taper off unfinished.

Hank looked in his mug and saw it was almost empty. He tipped back the cup and downed the last of the coffee before placing it on the nightstand.

"Take another bite, dear," he said, figuring she would follow it with another sip.

Her head lolled before her eyes settled on the tray. She reached out slowly and picked up the toast, tearing off a small portion with her teeth. She replaced it on the plate and lifted the mug, taking another drink.

"Mmmm," she said.

Hank wondered if it meant something, or if it was merely the drug's effect.

As she took another sip, the mug slipped from her grasp, spilling a dribble of coffee on her chest, darkening her nightdress. Hank stood and grabbed the cup. Now almost empty, he placed it on the nightstand next to his own.

"Sorry," Eliza said, giving an unfocused stare.

"No worry." He dabbed the coffee stain with his napkin.

"I...feeh...tire..." Eliza muttered, almost incomprehensibly.

Lifting the tray, Hank folded the legs up and moved it back to the dresser. "Let's have you take a rest now, dear," he said, and he tilted her forward to remove the pillows before reclining her into a lying position.

Her glassy eyes gave no response, but they blinked slowly, like a contented cat's.

Hank's vision blurred as his eyes went watery. He brushed her hair with his fingers, arranging it so it flowed gracefully across the pillow. *Oh, my poor Eliza.*

He returned to the rocking chair and reached for her hand. Her arm twitched slightly as her eyelids rolled closed.

As the minutes slipped by, Eliza's labored breathing progressively slackened.

Tears trickled down both of Hank's cheeks, dropping into his lap. He squeezed his eyes shut, and a flickering image formed on the inside of his lids: Eliza, when they had first met at the grain operation office where she worked. Hank had made a few more visits than he really needed, but she always greeted him enthusiastically. When he finally got up the nerve to invite her to lunch, she smiled and said, "Of course," as if it was a silly question.

The memory of him carving H.M.+ E.S. inside a heart on the trunk of the giant pond-side elm tree flashed in his head. It was Eliza's first visit to the farm, three months after they started dating, within weeks of his marriage proposal.

Eliza gave a short gasp and her chest hitched, pulling Hank back into the present. Her faltering breaths had weakened to shallow gulps, punctuated by a rattle deep inside her lungs. The sound was something awful, like a stream of ball bearings dropping on concrete with every breath.

Hank began humming as a way of drowning out the dreadful rattle. Unable to think of anything but Christmas songs, he hummed "Silent Night," "Jingle Bells," and "White Christmas." Eliza had always loved Christmas carols, so he hoped some part of her might be comforted by hearing them. With the stress of the moment, those were the only ones he could think of, so when he finished, he cycled through them one more time.

As the minutes ticked by, stretching into an hour, other fragments of memories played out inside Hank's mind. He thought about the time when they had first moved into the house to take over the farm. Eliza had flipped a penny into the wishing well she loved so much, making a wish she never did disclose. "Wishes are secrets, Hank. If you tell them, they don't come true."

Glancing at Brenda's desk with tear-swollen eyes, Hank thought about how Eliza had beamed when they brought their newborn daughter home. She could not stop looking over the tiny infant, asleep in her cradle.

Hank grimaced, recalling how helpless he had felt after they lost Brenda. He had wanted so desperately to find some way to comfort Eliza, but instead, he withdrew, swallowed in his own despair. It was as if a part of him needed to detach in order to survive. As time slowly healed their wounds, guilt for having let his wife down in her time of need formed Hank's scar tissue.

At length, Hank realized Eliza's breathing had stalled and her hand had gone cold. He remained at her side, weeping, vaguely aware of the endless succession of clock ticks resounding from the dresser, somehow seeming louder as the morning slipped away, like reminding him his own time was running short.

Eventually, Hank felt he could cry no longer, and when he checked the time, was stunned to see it was well after eleven. He stood and placed Eliza's hand on the bed by her side. She'd gone slack-jawed, her head tilted back and cocked askew. He gently straightened her neck into a more comfortable-looking position and pushed her chin upward to partially close her mouth.

"Rest now, my love," he whispered before leaning over and kissing her cold forehead. "No more suffering."

While some might question whether mercy could ever be involved in the act of killing, at that moment, Hank Mitchell knew otherwise.

⸻◆⸻

The iron posts of the family plot's fence gate felt solid and cool in Hank's grasp, an antidote to the surreal sensations thrumming through his brain. *Is it really over?* The cluster of headstones before him drove home the finality of it all. The Deed was done, and there was no going back. How lonely would life be without Eliza? *Never mind that, Old Man. You've still got work to do.*

He turned around to face the house, then tilted back his head, clearing the bill of his hat from his line of sight to Eliza's bedroom window. This was his last chance to make her death official by calling an ambulance or a funeral home. Except, the danger was someone might do a toxicology test. There was no telling whether Xylazine would be detected, but was that a chance he would be willing to take?

Squinting at the window, Hank mulled over the alternative he'd been weighing. He lived in isolation, with no nearby neighbors. Eliza's family would not come looking for her, and *his* family had all died off. With the cemetery behind the house, nobody would even need to know.

Well, Pastor Lionel Burns might have his suspicions. Hank let out a huff. *Why did I talk to that man?* Still, a so-called spiritual leader would not go to the police, would he? And anyway, if Hank stayed out of Clarkton, there would be little risk of bumping into the minister, or anyone else who might start asking questions. He could persist on the farm for years...decades, if he lasted that long, without ever raising suspicions.

And now, there was another issue he had not previously anticipated: that wicked bruise on Eliza's face would surely trigger scrutiny. Hank chewed the inside of his cheek. He had been leaning in the direction of a secret burial, but this development seemed to clinch it.

A lonely existence was one thing; joining Doctor Death in prison for the balance of his life was something else altogether. Because *this* decision seemed trivial compared to the quandary of whether to perform The Deed, it was not hard for him to make a snap, almost nonchalant call.

So that was it. In Hank's mind, the fateful matter was closed by the time he turned back toward the cemetery.

As he stared at the spot where Eliza would be buried, he thought about how much work it would be to dig her grave. Beneath the upper layer of topsoil, the ground would turn to clay, with plenty of chunks of sandstone interspersed. But he could use the tractor's backhoe attachment to tear through the tough subsoil. He figured that filling it back in by hand would not be so hard once the earth had been loosened.

Eliza would be laid to rest beside her daughter. He studied the spot, gauging the distance in his mind between the fence and the foot of Brenda's grave. Would the backhoe reach over the wrought iron and out that far? *I reckon so.* If he was right, he could work from behind the graveyard and avoid removing a section of the fence. He shrugged. *It's worth a try.*

When he slid the barn door open, the feral cat fled, scooting further back into the interior. His John Deere tractor sat just inside the doors, and although he could not recall what he had last used the tractor for, he was relieved to see the backhoe implement was already attached. When he climbed up and turned the key, the diesel engine roared to life, the fuel gauge showing over half full.

He drove the tractor out the door and around the barn, passing the wildflower patch—their former garden—and through a drift of fallen leaves that had accumulated behind the barn. As he approached the back of the cemetery, he swung the tractor around, climbed out, pushed the levers to extend the boom and the elbow so the backhoe would clear the fence, then crawled back in. He reversed the machine into position, behind the spot where Eliza would be laid to rest. After setting the feet, he returned to the backhoe seat and pulled the lever to bring the bucket down, releasing it when the teeth pierced the ground. He nodded when he saw it reached just far enough.

The machinery operation proved therapeutic, since it forced Hank to focus on something other than Eliza. He carefully peeled off the sod layer and deposited it above Brenda's grave, then clawed into the ground. Each scrape yielded a bucket load of dirt, which he dumped into an elongated pile on the opposite side.

Fifteen minutes in, the grave was cut, and he had scraped down to some unknown depth. Hank decided he would need to measure. He left the engine idling, slid out, and set off for the barn workshop to fetch a measuring tape.

When he stepped out of the barn and back into the sunlight, Hank froze. A rusty white station wagon was rolling down the gravel roadway, moving much too slowly for a typical passerby. With the idling tractor, he had not heard the car approach. As panic welled up in his mind, his first instinct was to duck inside the barn, but it was entirely possible he'd already been seen—as well as the backhoe he'd left amid its graveyard dig. He forced himself to hold his ground, knowing any attempt to hide would only draw more suspicion about his activities.

The car passed behind his house, and when it emerged on the opposite side, it accelerated, sending gravel spraying behind the rear wheels.

Who could this be? With its window rolled up, Hank could not see the driver. Vehicles rarely traversed the township road, since, aside from the valley's few households—or their visitors—there was simply no reason to follow this back-road route. He did not recall ever seeing *this* car before. Even the *type* of car looked out of place. A station wagon? Not very practical in these parts, where most of the vehicles were pickup trucks.

Hank stood still as a fencepost, watching while the car rolled onward. Halfway to Shirley Gould's house, when it had passed far enough that Hank could see both taillights, they blazed red. The car slowed to a crawl.

"Get the hell out of here," Hank said out loud. Beyond Shirley's house, the brake lights blinked off, the car sped up, and soon, it disappeared around the road bend. Hank waited for a minute or more, then told himself, *Get moving, Old Man.* At this point, he could not afford to spend time or energy worrying about what the driver had seen.

He opened the gate against its wailing, corroded hinges and removed his hat as he stepped inside.

When he reached the foot of the freshly dug grave, the awful reality hit him: Eliza would soon be lying in this hole. His throat clenched up. Pivoting back to face the farmhouse, he eyed the window of Brenda's room, where Eliza's body now lay.

He took in a heavy breath, turned away, stretched out the measuring tape, and steered the end down against the newly cut surface. Most of the hole checked in at two feet deep. He recalled debating the proper depth with the mortuary when they had prepared to bury Brenda. The funeral parlor informed him that while people often believed graves were dug to six feet in depth, the standard practice in Ohio was four feet.

Hank pocketed the tape measure and returned to the tractor.

On the very next scrape, the teeth caught on something, bogging the engine under the hydraulic load. *Tree root?* Hank wondered, but before he had a chance to second-guess why a tree root would be in this spot, the implement broke through the resistance, jarring the machine.

"Oh..." Hank said out loud when he saw a chunk of concrete lift from the hole. It was not a tree root. A sick feeling took hold in his gut with the realization he had broken off a piece of Brenda's burial vault. "Damn!"

He killed the engine and sat there, dreading the idea of a closer look. Smacking his thigh, he pushed out of the seat to investigate. As he hauled himself around the barn, he peered down the roadway, but there was no sign of the white station wagon.

Back at the open entrance gate, he pulled off his cap and trudged inside. His pace slowed as he approached the scar on the earth.

"Ohhh," he said, dropping to his knees at the foot of the open hole.

He had clipped the corner of her concrete burial vault with the excavator bucket, breaking it off when he scraped forward. From his position, the crevice revealed nothing but darkness, so he was at least relieved by that.

He crawled into the trench that would soon become Eliza's grave, then, while averting his gaze from the portal into Brenda's burial vault, hoisted the concrete chunk, puzzling it back into place. With his palms pressed against the piece of coffin liner, he took several heavy breaths.

"I'm sorry to disturb you, Brenda," he whispered. "I hope you understand about your mother. Maybe you're together now. She missed you so much." He blinked out a tear and sniffed, adding, "We both have."

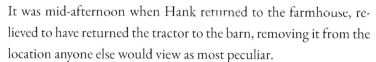

It was mid-afternoon when Hank returned to the farmhouse, relieved to have returned the tractor to the barn, removing it from the location anyone else would view as most peculiar.

He realized he had not eaten a thing since the single piece of toast, so he used that as an excuse to loiter in the kitchen for another half hour, putting off the task he was dreading. After looking through the pantry and refrigerator, he forced himself to eat a can of Vienna sausages with a glass of milk and another slice of toast, this time, slathered with peanut butter.

Having finished his light meal, Hank stepped into the dining room enclave and stared at the table. With room for six, four of the seats had place settings: one each for Jimmy, Pop, Ma, and Brenda. With a knot in his throat, he wandered over to the cabinet and took out a fifth set of dishes and utensils, arranging a setting for Eliza to join the others.

All the gut-wrenching emotions Hank had managed to keep at bay while working outside erupted when he ascended the stairs. A queasiness took hold in his stomach as he prodded himself down the hall. He held up near the end, bracing himself, before stepping into Eliza's doorway.

Hank had to force himself to look over at the bed. Eliza appeared as though she could be sleeping. Only she wasn't, and he knew it.

He traversed the floor, pausing between each step. The clock on the dresser ticked away in its unremitting cadence. The floorboards creaked when he passed the rocking chair. As he drew in while holding his breath, Hank found himself reaching out to touch Eliza's cheek with the back of his fingers, just below the purple bruise.

She's cold, he thought, yanking his hand away, as if he hadn't quite expected it.

Bursting into tears, Hank fell upon her, pressing himself against her body, feeling her lifeless cheek against his own. A minute later, he pulled himself away. Unprepared to leave Eliza's side, he crumpled into the rocking chair, sobbing, his face buried under his hands.

After half an hour passed, Hank wiped his nose and cheeks with his handkerchief, thinking, *Better get to it, Old Man. There's not much daylight left.* He squeezed the water from his eyes, dabbed them dry, and stood.

From the side of her bed, he uncovered Eliza, rolling the bedcovers down toward the footboard. He moved gently, feeling as though he had to avoid waking her, then choked up at the ludicrous thought.

Hank considered changing Eliza out of her nightclothes, and into something else, but decided against it. She would have viewed the process as humiliating, and anyway, it didn't matter.

He lifted the cover of her mostly empty wooden keepsake box on the dresser. Eliza never owned much in the way of jewelry, perhaps another outcome of her Amish upbringing. He plucked a silver broach from the box, then, with shaking hands, pinned it to her nightgown, above her heart, and just below the coffee stain. "You always loved this broach," he whispered. "Remember? I got you this for our fifth anniversary."

From the foot of the bed, he removed her treasured pink quilt, which he stretched out beside her on the opposite side. When he began lifting her to pull the quilt underneath her, Hank dropped her abruptly, recoiling. With his teeth clenched, he counted out ten of the nearby clock's ticks, then swallowed and reached out to clutch her wrist. When he tried to lift her arm, he found it had already gone rigid.

Rigor mortis.

The words bored into his skull like a drill bit. With one fist pressed against his lips and his other hand compressed against his chest, he took in a long, quivering inhale. After a few more ragged breaths, he shoved the repulsive realization aside and went back to work, wrapping her in the quilt from head to toe, but keeping her face uncovered for the time being.

When Hank was done, he checked the clock. It was after 4:30 p.m. Less than two hours of sunlight remained. But he wasn't yet ready. He sat on the rocking chair and rocked slowly, the floorboard creaking with each roll, a fluttering sensation in his heart.

A few lonely minutes later, he told himself, *It's time.*

He stood, bent over, and kissed Eliza's forehead. "Goodbye, my love." A drop of brownish foam had dribbled out of the corner of her mouth. After wiping it away with his hankie, he straightened her hair with his fingers and then pulled the quilt over her face.

The lump in his throat ballooned as he lifted Eliza's board-stiff body off the bed, but he fought back the tears. He navigated slowly into the hall and down the stairs, being careful to avoid bumping any part of her rigid limbs against the wall.

In the kitchen, Hank found he could hold her stiffened corpse with one arm, freeing the other to pick his hat off the hook and pull it onto his head. Although he normally removed his cap in the family plot, he would wear it for the task ahead.

He swung the screen door open and stepped out into the unseasonable warmth, which had lessened as the shadows grew long.

While he carried her across the lawn toward the family plot, Hank thought about how Eliza would have commented about the beautiful weather. *It doesn't get any better than this,* she might have said, or, *Now this is a perfect fall day.*

Inside the cemetery, he placed her on the ground beside her open grave, then descended at the foot, where he had carved a slope with the backhoe claw. After having damaged Brenda's burial vault, he had shifted his cut over eighteen inches from the original, ample berth to ensure he stayed clear of her coffin liner.

From the center of the grave, Hank reached under Eliza's rigid body, lifted her from the ground, and then lowered her to the bottom. He immediately saw that he had dug the grave considerably longer and wider than her slight frame required. He should have anticipated this since he'd been astonished at how much Eliza had shrunk in the past few months. She had been petite to start with, but it was as though she'd not only lost weight and muscle mass, but had somehow grown shorter in height as well.

Squatting over her, he smoothed the quilt over her head and torso, while the hollow ache in his chest intensified. "Goodbye, Eliza." He held her shrouded head with both hands and squeezed gently. "Rest in peace, my love."

With a trembling sigh, Hank pulled away and crept out. He knelt beside the hole, staring down at the cloaked figure, and with little warning, he burst into tears. His body lurched between sobs, a cascade of teardrops rolling off his face, pouring into the grave.

The sound of horses made him flinch, wrenching him out of his anguish. Just then, it dawned on him that the Amish men would be leaving the job site about this hour. Although he judged he should be fairly well hidden this far from the road, he didn't want to take any chances. He scrambled into the trench and crouched out of view, listening intently.

The clopping moved closer, and after passing his home, began to diminish. He poked his head up far enough to peer out, and counted the tops of seven buggies rolling away, at this point passing in front of Shirley Gould's house.

After they disappeared around the bend, Hank looked around. Shadows had stretched clear across the graveyard. When he suddenly grew aware that he was crouching in an open tomb with a corpse, he promptly clambered back out.

Standing at the foot of the grave, he checked his watch and discovered it was just after five o'clock. With the prospect of burying Eliza during sunset giving him the shivers, he headed to the barn to retrieve the shovel.

When he returned, he stood motionless beside the pile of dirt for a while, holding the simple spade that his father had owned long before him, its aged handle smooth and hard, the tip of the rusted steel worn flat. He considered saying a prayer. The notion offered a certain ritualistic appeal, but he eventually decided the raw emotions were enough, and went to work.

The loosened soil was not difficult to move. He made a point of dropping the clumps on either side of Eliza, but before long, the shovel loads began spilling onto her body, and soon the quilt was concealed under clods of dirt.

He diverted the stones as he came across them, pitching those smaller than the size of a skull into the nearby band of trees, while dropping the larger ones into a pile behind the fence, to be moved later.

When the spade gave an unusually sharp ring, Hank scrounged through the soil with the tip of the tool and discovered an Indian arrowhead. A fleeting thought formed in his mind: *Wait till Eliza sees this.* Then he caught himself, and the idea dissipated like a handful of sand streaming through open fingers. With a hard swallow, he bent down to collect the relic.

Rubbing the dirt off exposed color striations across a semi-glossy surface. Fashioned from the Coshocton gray flint that originated in nearby deposits, the artifact was similar to at least a dozen others he'd unearthed on the farm during his lifetime. Hank thought about whoever had created this item hundreds—perhaps a thousand years ago, and he sensed the presence of countless spirits who had come before him in the region. Suddenly feeling smaller and less significant, he dropped the arrowhead into his pants pocket and went back to filling the grave.

Soon, adrenaline surged within his body, fueling a quickening of his pace. He eventually stopped to rest when the hole was half-filled. With the shovel propped against his torso, he pulled his cap from his head and wiped the sweat away with the back of his sleeve.

With his hat back in place, Hank surveyed his surroundings. While he spotted nothing out of place, he detected a chipmunk, somewhere nearby, sounding the steady chucking noise the tiny rodents emit when facing an aerial predator threat. Hank tilted his head back and scanned the sky, finding no sign of a hawk. The critter carried on with its incessant warning calls, but after Hank went back to the burial, they soon faded into the background.

The grave was filled in less than an hour, leaving a raised rectangular mound that would settle with time. Hank spent a few minutes tamping the soil with his feet, then took to his hands and knees to piece together a patchwork of sod, blanketing Eliza's tomb in a living veneer.

Under the last glimmer of dying sunlight, he kneeled at the side of the mound, pressing both palms against the grassy hump. *It ain't right putting Eliza in a grave with no headstone.* But the fundamental problem was that he had buried her secretly, so didn't that mean he couldn't mark her grave? *How about a cross made with sticks? Forget about it, for now, Old Man. You'll have plenty of time to think it over.*

Overhead, bats darted silently across the darkening sky. The brightest stars were already visible, and within an hour, the vast streak of the Milky Way galaxy would be painted above the farm.

Hank noticed how chilly the dusk air had grown, the warmth slipping away with the sunlight. A shiver passed over him, partly triggered by the coolness, but undoubtedly largely a product of his emotional state.

He pulled himself up and gathered the shovel, then hesitated, staring at the mound near his feet. *Eliza's in this grave.* The reality of it felt like an ice pick to the brain. *Fifty-three years of marriage ends like this?*

Another round of tears leaked from his eyes as Hank pondered how profoundly his world was about to change. What would life be like without his wife? While he had felt all alone in his struggle to care for her over the past couple of months, the onset of *true* loneliness—*oppressive* solitude—squeezed him like a tightening vise. And now, with the impending isolation of winter, the farm's seclusion, the very thing he had always cherished, loomed as something to fear.

A wipe of his cheek with a dusty shirt sleeve left smears of grit on his face. He brushed it off, shifting his gaze to Brenda's headstone. Eliza was now resting beside their beloved daughter. *At least they're together now.* Reuniting them in the family plot at long last provided Hank with a glimmer of comfort.

Yet the bigger source of solace was knowing Eliza would not have to face any more fear or suffering. *It wasn't easy, but you did the right thing, Old Man. She needed you, and you took care of her...for one last time.* Except, there was a small part of him who was not so sure about that, wasn't there? *Perhaps, but that's to be expected.* If nothing else, at least he would no longer have to wrestle with the endless internal debate that had been raging inside his mind.

Hank was caught off guard by a sudden craving for a cigarette, which he had not experienced in years. He had kicked the habit in 1982—actually, he had quit so many times, he'd almost given up trying—but somehow, that time, it stuck. Eliza had always warned him: *You're going to get lung cancer, Hank.* How ironic was it that she was the one who ended up with cancer in the lungs when he was the one who had smoked for roughly half of his life?

The barn owl shrieked from the nearby stand of trees, snapping Hank out of his trance. He lifted the spade, turned away from Eliza's fresh, unmarked grave, and headed toward the cemetery exit.

CHAPTER 13

AFTERMATH

OCTOBER 15, 2002

H ANK MITCHELL AWOKE THE next morning to the sound of
horses and buggies. The clock read 7:45. The first sunbeams
were beginning to stream through the window, bathing the room
in daylight. He winced at his achy muscles and smarting back as he
pushed himself upright. *Should I be this sore?* he wondered. *Pfft. For
heaven's sake, you're 74!*

He let out a faint groan as he labored the short distance across
the room, then stepped to the side of the open window, concealing
himself behind the curtains.

A procession of seven buggies paraded past the house.

When Eliza drifted into the forefront of his thoughts, his knees
turned into Jell-O. For a fraction of a second, he wondered if it all
might have been a dream. But just like the tiny puff of smoke when
a candle is extinguished, the notion vanished. He leaned against the
wall, crushed by the gut-wrenching knowledge that his wife was
gone.

Hank decided then to visit her graveside. He steadied himself,
pushed away from the wall, and lumbered across the hall to the
bathroom. While standing over the toilet, he wondered, *When did*

I go to bed? He seemed to recall turning in early, but could not remember the time. *Nine o'clock? Ten?* He had no idea.

Trying to play it back in his head, he found that after burying Eliza, the balance of the evening was nothing but a blur. Almost as if he'd been sleepwalking, he had a foggy memory of heating a frozen Chicken Fried Steak with Gravy supper (Eliza's favorite). After forcing himself to eat a few bites, he covered it back up and stowed it in the refrigerator. That was his only recollection. It was like his brain function had been blunted after that. He concluded this was all his burned-out mind could absorb, and he went on with his morning cleaning and dressing routine.

Stopping at the bottom of the stairs beside Eliza's wheelchair, Hank rubbed his whiskers. *What should I do with this?* With a sigh, he wheeled it into the corner.

In the kitchen, he went about making coffee, but the choking sensation tightened when he told himself to stop adding water halfway to the residue ring.

Although hunger still eluded him, he knew he should eat, so he made himself a single piece of toast, plastering a layer of apple butter on it as the coffeemaker gave its final gurgle.

He gazed out the window above the sink as he nibbled on the toast and slurped the coffee. Bands of vibrant fall color filled the span of woods stretching along the western property line, ablaze with morning sun. The beautiful sight and the lingering warmth lifted Hank's spirits if only a tad.

When he finished the last bite of toast, he sluiced it down with another swig, wandered to the back door, pulled it open, and stepped up to the screen. He was taking another sip of his coffee when he froze, spitting the drink back into his mug.

What the hell?

He slanted forward and gawked across the yard to the cemetery, then pulled his head back and furrowed his brow as he tried to make sense of what he was observing. He blinked, not believing what his eyes were telling him, not wanting to accept what seemed to be so clear.

A mound of dirt was piled beside Eliza's grave.

With panic erupting in his throat, Hank ditched the mug on the kitchen table and flung open the screen door, stepping out onto the sandstone slab. Because of the property's upward slope, he could discern nothing unusual besides the out-of-place heap of dirt. Trotting across the short expanse of grass, he strained for a better view.

As he approached the gate, his heart turned into a marching band bass drum, slamming at a rapid tempo. He grasped the wrought iron posts to steady himself, his mind a violent tornado as it struggled to decode the unimaginable scene he could now see so clearly: Eliza's grave, an open fissure in the ground. But from where he stood, the floor of her tomb remained hidden from his line of vision.

He pulled his eyes away and scanned his perimeter with hitching breaths, searching for a presence that did not belong. He turned the opposite way, then spun around, frantically panning in all directions.

A squirrel stared at him from the grindstone-capped well, the only sign of life in sight. Off in the distance, a woodpecker jackhammered away on a tree, and somehow, Hank felt his skull vibrate with the racket.

He swung back around, braced for the sound of the squealing hinges, pivoted open the gate, and staggered inside. Quick strides carried him closer, and when he was halfway to the open scar of earth, the top end of the grave's bottom came into view.

The hole was empty.

Drawing in on the foot of Eliza's grave, a tidal wave of dizziness washed over Hank, and he stumbled as though he'd been punched in the face. When the last of his balance deserted him, his legs crumbled, and the ground rose to meet him.

He fought the vertigo threatening to overwhelm him. From his hands and knees, he leaned forward and peeked into the trench, sweeping through from the head end to the foot, like making certain he hadn't overlooked the body that should have been there. The vacant grave muted his guttural moan.

It was *impossible.*

Yet here it was.

Through ragged gasps, Hank slouched into a sitting position and pulled his knees up against his chest. "Eliza?" His voice cracked.

With sanity slipping from his grasp, his eyes flitted across his surroundings once more. But still, he saw no one.

Hank Mitchell burst into tears and cried, "Where are you?"

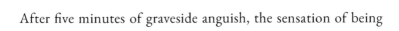

After five minutes of graveside anguish, the sensation of being watched crept over Hank.

He composed himself and scrabbled to his feet. Standing in place on unsteady legs, he scrutinized his surroundings. Unsure of what he was looking for, he examined all the little nooks where someone could be hiding: in the woods, the swales of the yard, the windows of the barn and house, and in the weeds growing along the road. When he completed the 360 without spotting anything, he questioned, *Am I* really *being watched, or just being paranoid?* He decided a patrol loop might help him find out.

But first, he studied the dirt, searching for footprint evidence. He soon gave up hope. Although the entire area had been trampled, there were no discernable markings. Hank had always believed that although footprints made good movie fodder, in the real world, it took unique conditions for a shoe to leave a clear identifying imprint. What he saw only confirmed his opinion.

He left the cemetery and edged along the western end of the yard, examining the open areas amongst the underbrush as he passed. Tracing across the front, he surveyed the full stretch of creek-side scrub beyond the roadway before halting at the eastern side of the lawn.

Unable to shed the feeling that he wasn't alone, Hank stared in the direction of Shirley Gould's house. The longer he looked that way, the more the unnerving sensation gathered strength.

Hidden behind the trees, the dwelling's nickname rattled inside his head: *Ghoul House.* The childhood memory of discovering the old woman's open grave gnawed at him. Now, somehow, the same twisted fate had befallen Eliza's tomb. Could there be some sort of curse on the house, which caused old ladies buried nearby to rise from the dead? With a shiver, Hank tore away his gape and resumed his trek, heading back along the eastern end of the lawn.

Behind the barn, he held up, carefully studying the outer fringe of the corn stand. *Between the stalks would be the perfect hiding place.* But as far as he could see, there was nothing unexpected there.

By the end of the loop, the sense of being watched diminished. Could it have been just his vulnerable condition? *Yeah, that's probably all it was,* he assured himself. He cleared his mind with a quick head shake and trudged back to the house.

Unable to decide what to do about this monstrous development, Hank holed up in the kitchen, lingering inside the open door. His brain went numb as he stared through the screen at the family plot, chewing the inside of his cheek.

Asian ladybeetles swarmed around the screen door's exterior. Hank focused on one, watching as it crawled along the perimeter of the door frame in its relentless search for a way inside. Not native to the United States, the orange insects had been introduced to control aphids, and over just the past couple of years, had become a mild nuisance in the region. They had earned the nickname "Halloween ladybeetles," since on warm October days like this they mobbed homes, seeking a crevice to slip through to survive the coming winter.

A lucky one squeezed through a tiny gash in the screen and took flight inside, buzzing past Hank's ear and continuing its suicide pilgrimage to the warmth of some light fixture, where it would become trapped and perish. He let it go, reflecting on how Eliza had grown to hate the spring-cleaning mess they caused. The annoying little bugs smelled nasty when crushed, but worst of all, sometimes they'd bite. Nothing like a deer fly, mind you, but still... Despite all that, under the current circumstances, Hank welcomed the pests' presence and the mildly therapeutic distraction their routine provided.

Something rattled behind him, tearing his attention away from the insects. He whirled around and froze, mouth hanging open, eyes darting about, but found nothing. After a minute of silence, he shrugged, swung back to face the screen door, and his thoughts returned to Eliza's empty grave. *Where is she?*

They had never found Shirley's remains—or any explanation of what had become of her. Was the same thing happening again in the neighboring cemetery, almost 70 years later?

You're in a real jam here, Old Man. Can't exactly call the sheriff now, can you? About the only thing he could think to do was to go hunting for Eliza. The barn was the first place he'd search. Looking over his shoulder at the kitchen counter, he spotted the Maglite flashlight. He would need that.

The rattle sounded again, a distant chattering, then dissipated. While Hank's heart began thumping, he wandered to the back of the kitchen and cocked his head.

Half a minute later, the chatter resumed for just a second. *The cellar,* he thought. Reluctantly, he stepped toward the opening and stared down into the darkness. All was still. He flipped the light switch, brightening the stairway. At the bottom, a few feet of dirt floor receded into shadows.

The rattle resumed, longer this time, and *definitely* coming from the pool of darkness.

Hank grabbed the top of the banister and held fast, fighting the urge to flee. "Eliza?" he called down into the murk.

A breathless moment later, the chattering sound returned, an unsettling metallic rattle, which crescendoed, then faded into silence.

His heart pounded into his ears. "Are you down there, dear?" Hank felt utterly foolish saying the word "dear," but he made himself say it, because in the logic of the moment, it *was* some version of Eliza down there.

The rattle started up once again, dying away after a few seconds ticked by. He snatched the hammer sitting on the ledge, hefted it over his head, and summoned the courage to descend. He plodded downward, skimming his free hand along the length of the banister, his leeriness ratcheting up with each step closer to the unknown.

Holding up near the bottom, he reached out and yanked down the string dangling from the ceiling light, bathing the immediate area in light.

The rattle sounded, louder yet, frighteningly close now. Hank clapped his palm over his mouth and scanned his surroundings, moving only his eyes. *Where is she?*

With the hammer raised above his shoulder, he took the final two steps and reached the dirt floor. He froze, holding his breath, waiting for the noise to resume. When it did, he rocked back on his heels, pinpointed its direction, and whirled aside to face it.

The pot of applesauce.

He had forgotten all about the applesauce, which he'd left here to cool. Suddenly, the lid rattled, and he reeled back.

What in Sam Hill?

He bent over and leaned forward to examine the aluminum container, but found nothing unusual besides the undulating cover. He reached out for the black handle on the middle of the lid and grasped it, tentatively pulling it upward.

A wave of wriggling maggots spilled out from the pot, pouring out onto the dirt floor.

"Yuck," Hank said aloud, shoving the cover back onto the pot, squishing a layer of grubs that had wriggled over the rim, before skittering away from the slithering maggots.

From a distance, he waited, gathering his wits, relieved to know there was a reasonable explanation for the strange sound, but mad at himself for having forgotten about the pot. When he had left the lid cocked open over a week prior, he'd practically invited flies to enter and lay their eggs, which soon hatched into larvae. The maggots had grown until their collective mass overfilled the pot, lifting and giggling the aluminum lid while he watched.

Hank pressed the cover down tight and grasped the pot using the handles on both sides. Grubs immediately crawled over his fingers, and he flicked them away as he lifted the vessel from the ground.

Like a boiling pot of maggot soup, he thought in disgust.

He stepped on some of the fleeing grubs, but he quickly realized the futility of killing more than just a few and gave up trying. He held the metal container out from his body while he ascended the steps, straining to ignore the sore muscles throughout his arms and shoulders, and the slithering sensations on his hands.

Hank dumped the pot into the grass, then used the hose sprayer to pressure wash the maggot-applesauce stew into the soil. He paused to step on the largest masses, then resumed the torrent.

A few minutes later, he had blasted away the bulk of the disgusting blend. After giving the pot and lid a final rinse, he set the mated pair on the porch steps, tucked in beside the trio of pumpkins.

As Hank was turning off the spigot, he heard gravel popping under a vehicle's tires, sending him into a brief throe of alarm. *Stay calm*, he told himself. He gaped down the road at the oncoming car, a silver Crown Victoria, now barreling past Shirley Gould's house, trailed by a swirl of road dust, and heading his way.

Acting casually, Hank mounted the porch steps, forcing himself to wave when he reached the top. The vehicle slowed, and the passenger window rolled down as it came to a stop in front of the farmhouse. Reverend Lionel Burns, the Clarkton Baptist Church pastor, leaned over from the driver's side, wearing what Pop would have called a "shit-eating grin."

Hank groaned to himself. He'd all but forgotten how the pastor had virtually promised to stop by. That had been almost two months ago. Why did he have to drop in today, of all days? But his arrival was more than just an inconvenience. The timing was utterly weird, right? Hank narrowed his eyes and glared at the pastor, while a question crystallized in his mind: could this man have anything to do with Eliza's empty grave? Could the pastor be toying with him? With a little head shudder, Hank peeled away his glower. The idea was absurd; this was surely nothing but a strange coincidence.

"Are you up for a visitor?" Lionel Burns called across the yard.

Hank froze while his brain scrabbled for an out, only to come up empty. He shrugged as a sinking feeling developed in his gut. "I'm pretty busy today...but I suppose a quick visit would be okay."

The pastor nodded, and the car resumed onward while the window rolled up, before turning into the driveway.

Hank waited on the porch as the Crown Vic pulled up the drive. A sudden jolt of panic flashed through him when he realized he had to prevent the pastor from parking behind the house, where he might gain line of sight to the out-of-place mound of dirt in the family plot. He raised his hand in a "halt" sign, and the vehicle stopped. Releasing a sigh of relief, Hank nodded and gave a thumbs-up. Lionel Burns killed the engine and squirmed out.

"Nice pumpkins," the pastor said from the foot of the stairs, his eyes pausing on the pot accompanying them on the step. "Those are some unusual shapes."

"Thanks. Brenda taught me to look for oddball ones."

The minister extended his hand as he climbed the steps, and the men shook.

Hank was the one who broke the handshake. He motioned to the metal porch chair Eliza had abandoned when she relocated permanently into the wheelchair. "Can I get you something to drink? Coffee? Dr Pepper?"

"Oh, no thanks." Lionel Burns lowered himself into the seat. "After this, I'm heading to the hospital, where they'll fill me up with all sorts of beverages. I'll be floating out of there."

Hank situated himself in the swing, wondering how this was going to play out.

An awkward silence fell between the men as they both stared off into the yard. It was the pastor who finally broke it. "Beautiful day." He leaned over and looked up at the sky, making a show of admiring it. "Not a cloud up there."

Hank nodded. "Just the right temperature, too." He wanted to fiddle with his hat, but having left the house in such a hurry, he didn't have it. Instead, he swayed the porch swing gently.

Silence returned after the weather talk tapered off until Lionel Burns cleared his throat. "How's Eliza been?"

There it is. This was, of course, the obvious question.

Hank kept his gaze fixed on the front yard and beyond. "She's holding her own."

After a long half a minute passed, Hank turned back to Reverend Burns, who was staring at him intently. Realizing what else the man was likely wondering, Hank added, "She's upstairs...napping."

Pastor Burns nodded. The men sat quietly for a few moments before the minister spoke again. "I want to share something with you, Hank. It's a passage from the Bible."

Hank's stomach pitched. He dreaded hearing readings from the Bible, which usually made little sense to him.

Ignoring the lack of a reaction from Hank, the preacher reached inside his jacket and pulled a small, well-worn book from his inner pocket. "Would you like to read it, or should I?"

"Please, Reverend Burns. You can have the honor." Hank did not intend for his answer to carry a hint of sarcasm, but he felt like that's how it came out.

If the pastor took it that way, he gave no indication. He simply opened the small book to the page he had marked, pulled his reading glasses out of his front pocket, and slid them over his nose.

"This is the book of Job," he said, pausing briefly before continuing, but not waiting long enough for a response from Hank about whether that meant anything to him. It did not, though.

> "The sound of dread is always in his ear: and when there is peace, he always suspecteth treason. He believeth not that he may return from darkness to light, looking round about for the sword on every side. When he moveth himself to seek bread, he knoweth that the day of darkness is ready at his hand. Tribulation shall terrify him, and distress shall surround him, as a king that is prepared for the battle. For he hath stretched out his hand against God, and hath strengthened himself against the Almighty."

When he finished, Reverend Burns lifted his head and removed his reading glasses before peering silently across the lawn, a sort of dramatic flourish, like he'd just finished a reading in church.

Hank felt stupid, having gotten all tripped up over indecipherable words like "hath" and "shall." He waited for the explanation he was sure would follow.

"This passage got me thinking about you, Hank. The situation you're in."

If only you knew, Hank thought. He remained quiet, figuring the man would continue without prompting.

Pastor Burns closed the bible and put it back in his pocket. "What the bible says about Job reminds me of you, and the difficulties you're facing."

Hank held fast to his silence as he stared down at his lap. He suddenly spotted a stray maggot crawling across the inside seam of his thigh. Using one swift, casual motion, he surreptitiously brushed it off, as if it was nothing but a tiny ant.

"You can find strength in the Lord, Hank."

No sooner had the man's words registered, Hank felt a sensation on his stomach, under his shirt. *Another maggot?* He pictured a dozen grubs wriggling over his skin, having worked their way inside his clothes. *Get a grip on yourself, Old Man! Don't let your imagination run wild.* Perhaps that's all it was...his imagination. But still...

"You mustn't stretch out your hand against God, Hank."

Hank's focus shifted back to the minister, and more specifically, to what he was saying. If he understood correctly, the pastor seemed to be likening him to a man embracing sin. And the implication was he lacked faith—like he just should have *prayed* a little harder, or something.

Fighting to quell the sudden spark of anger, Hank turned away and locked his gaze on the pumpkins, as if they were important. He did not consider what he'd done to be a sin. Bringing an end to Eliza's suffering had been a difficult moral decision, and despite the horrific turn of events that followed, he *still* felt conviction that he'd done the right thing.

Of course, the pastor did not see it that way—he *couldn't* see it that way.

Bite your tongue, Old Man. Nothing good can come from arguing. Best to wrap this conversation up and get back to the issue at hand: finding Eliza. Hank drew in a long breath of air before turning back to his unwelcome visitor. "Appreciate your concern, Reverend. But don't worry. I'll be strong for Eliza."

The preacher squinted at Hank and nodded before turning away. Neither man spoke for a stretch.

Eventually, Hank interrupted the lull in their conversation. "Reverend?"

Pastor Burns's eyes met Hank's.

"Can I ask you a question?"

"Of course, Hank."

"Have you told anyone?"

Lionel Burns gave him a questioning look. "About what?" It was all almost like an act of innocence.

Hank hesitated, working out what words to use. "About our discussion."

"Heavens, no. That's between us. Well, actually...it's between you and the Lord."

Hank studied the minister. He had said the words earnestly and seemed to be genuine. But could this man, whom he'd made the mistake of confiding in, have something to do with Eliza going missing from her grave? Hank kept his eyes locked on Lionel Burns. "Did you tell anyone else that Eliza ain't doing well?"

The pastor looked away and stared in the direction of his car. Either he was dodging the question, or trying to recollect. Which was it? When the man turned back to Hank, he did a quick head shake. "Not that I recall."

Hank paused before responding, "I'd rather you didn't, frankly. We ain't looking for sympathy, you know?"

Reverend Burns gave a flustered smile, then mumbled, "I under-stand."

The men went mute for at least a minute until Hank found his voice. "Well, I'd best be getting on with my chores. Eliza will be waking up before long."

The pastor pushed himself out of the seat and extended a hand. "And I'd best be on my way, anyway."

"Thanks for your concern, Reverend Burns."

"Give my regards to the missus?"

With Hank's nod, the preacher turned to leave. As he descended the porch stairs, he said over his shoulder, "You folks be sure to enjoy this fine weather. There won't be many more days like this before winter starts knocking on our door."

Hank leaned against the porch rail as the pastor shimmied into his car, started it, and backed down the drive.

Never should have opened up to that man, Hank thought. He'd been seeking moral and spiritual guidance, but the minister saw the world as only black or white, whereas Hank could see shades of gray in between.

The pastor waved as the Crown Vic departed, leaving a dust cloud in its wake.

Hank Mitchell shuddered when he felt the unmistakable sensa-tion of a maggot crawling on his chest.

Stark naked, Hank hurried through the house for the shower, having left his clothes in a pile outside the back door. After locating half a dozen maggots inside his shirt and pants, he was not willing to risk overlooking any others. He leaned under the shower head even before the water had warmed up.

The shower provided a brief respite from his avalanche of disturbed thoughts, but the momentary serenity soon fell away. He dressed hastily, preparing for his search. First, he'd check the barn. If someone had dug Eliza up, that seemed like the most logical place they'd have hidden her body, assuming they hadn't hauled her off.

Leaning against the edge of his bed, he let out an audible grunt when he bent over to pull his clean pair of pants on. Although his leg muscles were sore, his upper back and shoulders protested the loudest.

If Eliza didn't turn up in the barn, he'd have a look around the Gould house. After all, he could not shake the idea of some connection between Shirley's and Eliza's empty graves.

Ghoul House.

Hank let out a little groan as the moniker resurfaced in his brain.

When he stepped out of his room, he glanced down the hall, noticing that Eliza's door was closed for the first time. *That's strange. Did I shut it yesterday?*

He turned that way and proceeded to the opposite end of the corridor. As he drew in, he saw the door wasn't completely closed. He reached out and pushed it wide open. The hinges creaked as it swung.

When the room came into view, a bolt of shock struck Hank in the forehead, almost knocking him off his feet. He regained his balance by clutching both sides of the door frame. Standing in the doorway with his mouth hanging open, Hank felt himself turn pale as he struggled to process the incomprehensible scene: Eliza lying on the bed.

Hank Mitchell strained to right his tilted world. A cyclone of troubled questions raged in his head. First, he wondered if Eliza was actually there, or if he'd conjured a psychotic mirage. Surely, his eyes were betraying him. He blinked, but the ungraspable image before him did not change.

Is she...alive?

Her eyes were closed. She did not move.

His mind reeled, groping about for some explanation.

Did I really *bury her?*

Maybe not. Perhaps it had all been a delusion. Could it be he hadn't even performed The Deed? Maybe she was merely sleeping.

It was the dirt-smeared quilt that shattered those hopes.

"What is all this?" Hank's question came out as a whisper to no one.

A wave of faintness doused him. He clawed the doorjamb to steady himself, his chest heaving as time ground to a halt. *Get a grip on yourself, Old Man. You're hyperventilating.* He focused on taking deep, calming breaths while bracing himself against an onslaught of emotions.

Wrenching his gape away from the horror inside the bedroom, Hank's neck grated as he turned to look over his shoulder, down the hall, searching for signs of an accomplice to this atrocity. The door had not been locked overnight. Heck, the deadbolt hadn't been turned since he was a child when Jimmy had lost the sole key. There had never been a worry about intruders.

Until now.

"Hello?" Hank's voice cracked. "Who's there?"

The clock on the nearby dresser clicked steadily, serving as a fragile mooring to reality. But nobody answered, and nobody appeared. He swiveled his head back.

It was just him. And Eliza.

Except...was it really *Eliza?*

"What...*are* you?" The horrible question spilled out of his mouth before he even had a chance to think about it. Once it was out, he could only hold his breath and wait.

The Eliza-thing gave no reply.

Of course it was Eliza, the logical part of his brain asserted. Her corpse, that is. The question was, how did it get here?

Hank's eyes began to sting, but he squeezed the feeling away, determined not to crack open the tear spigot. *Stay strong. And think.* With an audible exhale, he scanned the floor, searching for footprints, but spotted none.

Check her, he urged himself. But even as he thought this, he was turning away, preparing to flee, moving on reflex. He caught himself and held his ground.

He counted ten seconds inside his head while summoning the will to approach the bed. When he no longer felt like he was about to totter, Hank edged into the room, pausing inside the doorway with one hand on the dresser. After a dozen more clicks, he propelled himself toward Eliza, skulking, as though he needed to avoid waking her. The floorboard creaked when he stepped beside the rocking chair. Hank flinched, even though he was expecting it. Eliza remained utterly still.

Two more steps brought him to the edge of the bed. With his pulse thumping in his temples, he touched the soiled quilt she laid upon, the tactile sensation in his fingertips anchoring him against the madness.

With two sideways shuffles, Hank drew in on the headboard, within easy reach of Eliza's face. But he froze, swallowed in a daze, having lost command of his trembling hands. After considerable effort, he broke free and reached for her cheek. Upon touching her, he immediately withdrew his hand, knowing instantly from the coldness of her skin she could not be alive. Although he wanted to scream, his windpipe constricted so tightly he could barely even draw breath.

Eliza's pink quilt had been folded open, its outside caked in dirt, although she herself wasn't dirty. The silver broach he had pinned on her nightgown sparkled, just below the coffee stain on her night-dress. But her skin had turned a ghastly pale, aside from the bags under her eyes and the bruise on her cheek, both of which had dark-ened. Her eyeballs appeared sunken. Tiny brown smudges caked the corners of her mouth and lined her lips where they met.

She was *definitely* dead.

During several pounding heartbeats, Hank found himself won-dering if he was relieved by this conclusion, before deciding it made no difference. Either way, the situation was equally terrifying.

Just then, Hank envisioned something lurking under the bed, preparing to grab him by the ankles. In a swell of panic, he staggered out of harm's way and sunk into the rocking chair, gaining a clearer view of the hidden space. *Nothing there.*

A paralyzing sense of dread enveloped him. He raked his fingers over his face, wanting to flee from the hideous scene, but knowing he couldn't. He alone was responsible for Eliza's death, and that re-sponsibility carried a burden that robbed him of any right to escape.

Pull yourself together, he told himself, then nodded in response.

Hank sat back in the rocking chair, grappling with the question of how Eliza's body had gotten out of the grave and back here.

His thoughts shifted back to Shirley Gould, whose own body had somehow deserted the grave. Could the two cases be related? Except, Shirley didn't end up back in her home. Heck, he, Jimmy, and Pop had been in her house after she'd gone missing from the grave, and they would have seen her corpse if it had been there. The authorities had searched all over, including the one spot the boys hadn't dared to enter: the empty dwelling's cellar.

Maybe Eliza's haunting me. As he stared at her lifeless face, it suddenly seemed plausible that she had returned from the dead. Nothing like this ever happened with Brenda, though. Nor Billy, for that matter, or any of the other relatives buried in the family plot.

But you didn't murder *any of them.*

Hank sucked in a sharp inhale and tilted his head back, fixing his gaze on the ceiling. *Maybe Eliza's punishing you for what you did.* He told himself to look for a certain book in the parlor when he headed downstairs, hoping it might provide some clues.

Leaning forward, he steepled his fingers in front of his face, pressing them against his lips. *Focus, Old Man!* He strained to think rationally. Maybe the supernatural wasn't at play here...

Could this be some sort of sick Halloween prank? Like the most devilish gag imaginable?

But nobody knows...

Pastor Lionel Burns. The name entered Hank's mind as if somebody whispered it into his ear, and a queasy, fluttering feeling in his stomach immediately followed. *Damn—I should've never talked to that man.*

Okay, so maybe Reverend Burns knew what Hank had been contemplating. But even so, would the minister have done *this*? Why would he?

To taunt me. Torment...to make me pay.

And the preacher wasn't the only possible culprit, was he? This week—of all weeks, the valley was crawling with outsiders, with the Amish houses being raised just down the road.

In a snap, an image of the rusty white station wagon mushroomed inside Hank's head. He'd all but forgotten about how this car had passed through, slowly, while the backhoe sat in position for the cemetery dig.

Hank Mitchell let out a long, tortured moan and buried his face in his hands.

⚬

Hank located the book on the parlor bookshelf, flanked by a dozen VCR tapes on one side and several years' worth of *Reader's Digest* on the other. Not having looked at it in ages, he studied the paperback's cover:

OHIO GHOSTLY ROAD TRIP
The Most Haunted Houses in Every County

He had heard about the book when it was first published in the 1980s and bought a copy as a keepsake. The book described at least one allegedly haunted house in each county, although Homer County featured two entries: The Harmon Manor, nicknamed "Misery Mansion," which had once stood in the eastern end of the county, and the Gould homestead, now part of the Mitchell property.

Hank thumbed through to the Gould homestead entry, which featured an old photograph of Shirley Gould's house, taken before part of the roof had collapsed. He read the passage:

Tucked away off a remote gravel road in the southwest
corner of the county, you'd never know what horrors lie
concealed within this unassuming abandoned farm-
house. Legend has it that the last resident of the home,
Shirley Gould, went mad there in the early 1900s and
murdered her husband. It is said his spirit returned to
kill her in revenge. Found dead in her home, Shirley
was buried beside her husband in the small family
plot behind the farmhouse. But later, Shirley's grave
was discovered to have been opened, and her remains
were nowhere to be found. Folklore says Shirley's corpse
crawled out like a zombie, spawning a new nickname
for the Gould homestead: Ghoul House. Might Shirley
still be roaming the countryside as a ghoul, looking
for her next victim? Nighttime visitors claim to hear
a woman wailing from within the creepy old house.
Maybe it's the ghost of Shirley Gould they're hear-
ing. But perhaps it's not her ghost...maybe it's undead
Shirley. Beware of Ghoul House!

Hank closed the book and slid it back onto the bookshelf. Until today, he figured it was all just a bunch of nonsense, like the book was written for the entertainment of kids, rather than providing any serious account of inexplicable occurrences. Now, he was no longer as sure of that as he wanted to be.

While staring at the spine, Hank considered the god-awful developments of the past couple of hours, and he found himself wondering if there could be some truth behind what he had always considered mere silliness.

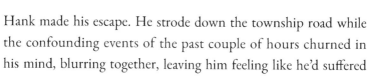

Hank made his escape. He strode down the township road while the confounding events of the past couple of hours churned in his mind, blurring together, leaving him feeling like he'd suffered through the darkest dream ever conceived. Except he knew he wasn't dreaming. Everything was too vivid, too cohesive for that. Nothing was muddled like dreams always are. Tragically, this was all very real.

Along his way, glimpses of the old Gould farmhouse began peeking through the autumn leaf cover. By the time he reached what had once been the driveway to Shirley's home, he found himself staring down the ancient structure. *C'mon, Old Man.* He tore his glare away, assuring himself, *It's just an old house.*

Near the spot in the ditch where the injured buck had fallen, Hank turned off the opposite side of the road and followed a narrow trail into the brush, down the bank to the edge of the creek. As a youth, this had been a favorite spot of his for catching tadpoles, crayfish, and salamanders, and years later, Brenda had carried on the tradition here. Somehow, the trail remained, the vegetation now slashed and trampled by the foot traffic of the deer, coyotes, and raccoons who maintained it.

Crows, which tended to congregate in this densely wooded stretch of creek, cawed ominously in the branches above Hank. The bird's cries dredged up a memory of the day when Jimmy had brought him into this area to explore for the first time. The crows had called eerily from above, putting young Hank on edge with fright. All these years later, the cawing sounds still had a way of unnerving him, although, with the terrifying events of the day, the effect now seemed trivial.

Hank traversed the creek by stepping on the dry tops of the stones protruding above the stream's surface. Panicked minnows darted away from the area where he crossed, seeking refuge in more distant pools of water. When he reached the opposite side, he lowered himself onto a gently sloping spot on the bank, covered by a spongy mat of creeping feather moss and a blanket of newly fallen foliage.

More autumn leaves dropped from the branches above, flitting in the air along their downward journey, giving Hank the soothing impression he was lying inside a snow globe. This spot would serve as a retreat...a temporary escape from the hellish situation at home. Hank had never been a drinker, but if he had been, he'd be pickled by now. Numbness in a bottle. *That might work better, I reckon. But, I'll make do with this.*

Soaking in the warmth—it felt more like mid-August than mid-October—Hank's thoughts strayed back to Shirley Gould's house. He lifted his head and eyed what he could see of the decaying dwelling through the brush, chewing his lower lip as he looked it over.

The gable facing his own house had collapsed, leaving the roof smothering the structure on that end. Standing out in sharp contrast against the gray siding, the two black window openings appeared like empty eye sockets, peering out through the gaps in the trees surrounding the home, with the window on the collapsed end compacted into an impudent wink. Hank looked away as the impression gave rise to goosebumps.

By the time Hank became intrigued with the spooky old farmhouse at eight years of age, it already looked to him as if it had been abandoned for decades. Would that eight-year-old boy have believed the house would still be standing all these years later? It was uncanny, really. Half a century ago, Shirley's home had already deteriorated to the point of being unsafe to enter, yet today the ruins still mostly stood, burrowed amongst the trees and vines that were seemingly consuming it. Sort of like it had some unearthly ability to endure.

When he turned to study the dilapidated dwelling once again, his thoughts wheeled back to the folklore surrounding it. *Ghoul House.* As a boy, he had lived in fear of the abandoned structure, and through the years had thought of Shirley as a witch, a ghost, or a zombie. While those childhood terrors had subsided decades ago, he now felt them encroaching into his mind once again. Ages had passed since he'd even considered the possibility of ghosts in Shirley's home. Could the supposedly haunted house somehow be involved in Eliza's return from the grave? Now, having found himself plunged into this living nightmare, the concept of supernatural influences on the world suddenly seemed conceivable.

He pushed aside the chaotic ruminations and stared at the bubbling water for a while, then dropped his head and closed his bleary eyes. Reflections on his boyhood triggered thoughts about how much time had passed since then. He felt stunned at how quickly it had rolled by, and how the years seemed to have accelerated as he aged. While he used to think of his grandfather as old, Hank had been surprised to realize he had outlived him—and Pop, too. For some time, he had comprehended that he was in the twilight of his life, but his head was spinning about how everything had changed in just a few months...and now Eliza was gone.

She *was* gone, right?

With a heavy sigh, he strived to clear his mind, focusing on the hypnotic reverberation of the stream, which soothed his battered psyche. The adrenaline had drained from his body, leaving him fatigued. Before long, on the comfortable padding of the moss, sleep dragged him away.

———————◄●►———————

Eliza returned again in Hank's dream. *My wife came home,* he thought to himself, but when he turned to look at her, he flinched in revulsion.

Eliza gazed blankly ahead, her eyeballs cloudy and devoid of life. Her wrist leaned on the arm of the porch swing, her lank hand dangling over the side. Covered in dirt, wild tangles filled her hair, clumps of soil clinging to the knots. The muddy streaks smeared across her face and hands couldn't mask the mottled grayness of her rotting flesh.

As he gently rocked the swing, her head bobbed up and down, like a bobblehead doll perched on a car's windshield dash, always nodding yes to questions no one asked. She made no other movements, merely staring ahead with a hollow death glare, her head swaying atop a limp neck.

My corpse wife.

Hank swallowed. "Are you okay, dear?"

She nodded, but slowly answered, "I'm so cold," her voice strangling through a throat clogged with dirt.

The skin on Hank's arms crawled. "You're cold?"

Another nod.

Something skinny flicked out from her mouth and squirmed in front of her teeth. Hank stopped swinging, leaning forward for a closer look. An earthworm.

"It's so cold." The worm wriggled free and plopped into Eliza's lap. "It's so...dark."

Even in his dream state, the weight of it all pressed down upon him with suffocating intensity, crushing him into the ground. Looking away, Hank Mitchell asked himself, *What have you done, Old Man?*

———◆◇◆———

It was the sound of crunching gravel that awakened Hank, initiating a slow transition from slumber into consciousness. In his struggle to rouse himself, he crouched forward and rubbed his face, then looked to his side for Eliza. When he discovered her gone, he came to the realization he'd been dreaming. He blinked hard, working to push the nightmare aside and secure a grip on reality.

The piercing black eyes of Ghoul House leered at him through the trees, while a single crow carried on, cawing from above. He tilted his head back and checked the sun's position in the sky, judging it to be well past mid-day.

The popping gravel sound resumed, and movement caught Hank's eye. He watched through the brush with sleep-blurred vision as a rusty white station wagon rolled slowly toward his cloistered location, after having halted near the driveway of Shirley's home. It passed his hiding spot, then skidded to another stop, where it idled unevenly for a stretch, a muffler hole giving it a throaty rumble. Then the engine revved, and the wheels spun on the gravel as it moved on, disappearing from view behind the thickening cover of undergrowth between the creek and the road.

The car struck Hank as familiar, but in his haze, he couldn't immediately place it. He massaged his eyes while striving to rid his head of cobwebs. Then it clicked, and his eyes shot open as a jolt of fury swept through him. *Who the hell is that?* Occasionally, unfamiliar vehicles will pass through on the country road, but did they ever return? Not likely. Why would they? Except this one had. Without a doubt, this same vehicle had come by yesterday—while he was in the midst of digging Eliza's grave.

Disregarding the protests of his aching muscles, Hank pushed to his feet, pausing for a spell to steady himself while the car drove away, the leaky exhaust sound growing distant after rounding the bend.

He hopscotched over the stones to cross the creek, but his foot skidded off the final moss-slickened rock and splashed before impacting the solid creek bottom beneath a few inches of water. He righted himself promptly, leaping to dry ground before the water could soak through his boot, then scampered up the embankment. But by the time he had reached the road, the vehicle had fallen out of earshot. Only the faint cloud of road dust the tires had coughed up remained, drifting into the woods lining the roadway.

Hank stood there for a few minutes, periodically switching his gaze between the vacant roadway and Shirley's house. He began scratching at itchy bumps that had sprouted on his arms, neck, and face, and he realized he'd been the source of a mosquito feeding frenzy while he slept. "Nasty creatures," he muttered, noting that if he had not been so distracted, he would have thought to spray himself with repellent before wandering into the thicket. He swatted at one buzzing in his ear, then turned and set off for home.

As he trudged down the road toward his house, Hank's head began to clear. He badgered himself with questions along the way. Who was driving this rusty white station wagon? Why had they come through two days in a row? And even more to the point: could this stranger have anything to do with Eliza's return from the grave?

Stalling at the foot of the veranda's steps, Hank took in the sight of the porch swing upon which Eliza had been sitting—in some sort of zombie state—in his dream. The despairing question he had asked himself echoed in his head: *What have you done, Old Man?*

He looked away. When he glanced at the trio of pumpkins, he noticed a pile of fallen leaves had accumulated between them. He took a moment to clear them out while asking himself a different question: *What did I do to deserve this?*

Except...you know *the answer, don't you?*

With a huff, Hank mounted the steps and headed for the front door.

Still rattled by the nightmare, Hank slipped into the parlor tentatively, conscious that his wife's corpse occupied the house, making him feel like an intruder. He pushed the door closed gently and turned to face the clock. It was after three. With most of the day having already passed, guilt for neglecting his responsibility bloomed inside him.

You need to rebury Eliza. Can't exactly leave her be.

But he had barely eaten. *I need energy.* Gladly taking the excuse to put off the grim task a little while longer, Hank traipsed into the kitchen.

He dropped into his usual seat at the dinette and arranged the leftover Chicken Fried Steak with Gravy supper and a cold can of Dr Pepper on his placemat. As he lifted the can for a swig, the icy sensation on his fingers reminded him of Eliza's words: "I'm so cold." He swallowed a sip and took a nibble of dry potatoes as he stared at the gap across the table, where Eliza's seat had been cleared to make way for the wheelchair.

Chewing slowly, he turned his gaze up to the ceiling. The bedroom where she lay was situated just beyond.

I'm so cold.

A few bites later, Hank checked the clock on the wall. It was now approaching 3:30. Yesterday, the Amishmen had passed through around five p.m., so he needed to avoid working in the graveyard during that time. But he also did not want to face the prospect of burying Eliza as dusk approached, like he had done the day prior. If he acted now, he figured he could finish before the Amish men came through. He slugged down what was left of his pop and pushed himself up from the kitchen table.

Upstairs, Hank's mouth went dry as he willed himself toward the doorway at the end of the hall. He had left Eliza's bedroom door ajar, troubled by the notion of her being alone and out of view. With a fist held tightly against his mouth, he held up in the hallway and slowly peeked in. Eliza remained just as he had left her. Still, he tarried for a handful of breaths, watching to see if she might sit up and leer at him. She remained motionless.

A tourniquet tightened around his heart as Hank moved in, fixing his gaze on Eliza. His pulse throbbed in his ears, all but drowning out the ticking clock behind him. The floorboard creaked when he stepped beside the rocking chair, jarring him out of his thoughts.

As he pressed in against the side of her bed, he wondered if he should have covered Eliza's face earlier in the day. *Ain't that what you're supposed to do with the dead?* But he somehow felt better seeing her uncovered. The skin on her face looked more ashen than it had in the morning. *Or is it just the lighting?* He reached out and touched her cheek with two fingertips.

Cold.

It's so cold.

Hank dropped into the rocking chair and ran both hands through what was left of his thinning hair. "I've got no idea what's happening, Eliza." Although he was ashamed of the tremor in his words, hearing the sound of his voice unspooled some tension from his nerves. He rocked backward, and the floor creaked. "Why are you here, and not in your grave?"

Eliza gave no reply.

"I reckon I need to bury you again. I don't know what else to do." A wary voice inside his skull responded, *She ain't here. Something else might be listening.* Hank's skin prickled at the suggestion. He narrowed his eyes and studied her for a spell before his gaze moved on, flicking about the room.

With a shake of his head, he let go of the breath he'd been holding and stood. Lifting one corner of the dirty quilt, he wavered for a while before cloaking Eliza's face underneath it. He tucked the length of the bedspread down her torso, then folded over the opposite side, forming a cocoon. When he lifted her from the bed, he saw that her body had lost most of its rigidity.

With rigor mortis waning, Hank found it easier to maneuver Eliza through the doorway and down the hall. Despite the strain on his sore muscles, she seemed lighter than the day prior, which helped further.

He swung open the rear screen door and stepped into the warmth. "It's still Indian Summer." He breathed the words into the shrouded bundle he hugged while traversing the lawn, pulling his face away when he caught a nasty whiff that reminded him of spoiled milk.

Hank slid down into a sitting position at the foot of the grave and cradled Eliza's corpse on his lap. He thought about what he was doing, weighing everything that had happened during the day. It was all so twisted, so unthinkable.

After a minute, he forced himself into action. He stepped forward, laid Eliza on the bottom, then fussed with the soiled quilt, smoothing and straightening it into a tidy shroud.

He pulled his hands away, stood, propped himself against the edge of the trench, and let his thoughts drift back to the quagmire he found himself in. Nearly breaking into tears, he cursed at the injustice of it all. How had the simple, normal life he'd shared with his wife so suddenly gone to hell? He longed for the peacefulness and contentment he'd taken for granted before everything went so horribly wrong.

With a groan, he pushed upright and ordered, *Get on with it.*

When he climbed out and stood over the hole, he mulled over whether to rebury Eliza by hand or use the backhoe. He decided to stick with the hand tool, reasoning it would not be hard to move the loosened soil, and not wanting to take the risk of someone seeing him doing backhoe work he'd be hard-pressed to explain.

After retrieving the spade from the barn, he went to work. When he began dropping shovel scoops of dirt into the grave, he could not help but feel that the burial seemed almost unceremonious on this go-around. He dissected it as he rhythmically moved one load of soil after another into the pit, the task lacking the emotional intensity it had carried the day prior. *It's almost like it's...routine...the second time around,* as strange as that sounded.

Perhaps "routine" was not the right word. It certainly wasn't like he didn't care. It was more like it had all become too much, so his brain had decided to transform into someone else, some uninvolved bystander, hired to do the dirty work. Then again, perhaps he was just weary, he surmised with an internal shrug.

As Hank worked, the inevitable question emerged: *Will she stay here?* His stomach felt like it was doing somersaults as he considered the taunting matter. *That's the real question, right, Old Man? Ain't that the worst part of this wicked affair?*

There was no denying it was. And if he did find Eliza back in the house in the morning, what would he do then?

Hank toyed with the notion of staying up all night, standing watch with the rifle, but he soon let the idea go. He had always been a regimented deep sleeper, so he knew how impossible it would be for him to stay awake—particularly in his current state of fatigue.

When the hole was filled, he carpeted the grave with patches of sod. Patting the last piece into place, he finally shed a tear, wondering if he did so out of a sense of obligation. *It just ain't right if I don't cry, is it?*

He squeezed his eyes shut and rubbed his fists against his temples. With the distraction of physical work over, Hank realized he had taken on a raging headache. The thought of a cigarette popped back into his mind, and he pictured a pack of Camels, his preferred brand. Considering the hell he'd been living through, he certainly deserved a smoke. What held him back more than anything was the half-hour drive to the closest store and the risk of running into someone he knew. *Don't go there,* he told himself, shaking the Camel pack image away and climbing up to his feet.

Hank did not linger in the family plot. After replacing the shovel in the barn and fetching his rifle, he checked his watch while stepping back into the late-day sunlight. It was just past five o'clock. Right on queue, the sound of horses and buggies arose when Hank mounted the sandstone slab at the back door, sending him scurrying into the house to avoid being seen.

CHAPTER 14

DESPERATION

OCTOBER 16, 2002

I T WAS NOT THE sound of horses and buggies or the early morning light that woke Hank up the next morning. Instead, it was the maddening itch of the mosquito bites. When he stretched and rolled over, the soreness in his muscles seemed worse than the previous morning. *Two straight days of grave digging will take a toll, Old Man. Or maybe your age is finally catching up with you.*

When he looked at the clock, Hank was surprised to discover it was 8:40 a.m. He had somehow slept through the Amishmen's arrival parade.

He recalled finishing the last of the Chicken Fried Steak with Gravy leftovers, then sitting listlessly in the parlor for a couple of hours in the evening, fighting off the incessant desire for a cigarette, until heading up for bed. The last thing he remembered was propping the rifle against the wall, within reach of the bed. Hank lifted his head and looked that way. The gun remained where he'd placed it. He had fallen easily into a deep sleep—the kind that leaves one feeling groggy upon awakening.

A hazy memory of a dream fragment lingered in Hank's mind, in which he had been lying on Eliza's bed, next to her corpse. He prayed she wasn't gone, but deep down inside, he knew better, and his mind was brimming with regret and sorrow. Now, staring at his closed bedroom door, he strained but failed to recall any broader context of the vague nightmare, or what followed. He shook his head to banish the disturbing recollection.

While he lay in bed working to clear his thoughts, Hank realized he was avoiding the dreaded task he would soon need to face: looking inside Eliza's room. *Will she be there?* The question brought a sinking feeling into his gut, making him want to curl up in a ball and forget the world.

Maybe this time Eliza stayed in the grave...where she belongs.

Or was that all just wishful thinking?

Pushing the covers aside, he rolled upright, swung his feet down to the floor, and stood, gritting his teeth against the body aches. After wrapping his plaid flannel robe around his body and sliding his feet into his slippers, he forced himself toward Eliza's room.

His heartbeat quickened as he proceeded down the hallway. *Will she be there?* The words echoed in his head.

As he stepped into the bedroom doorway, he reached for the doorjamb, tethering his grip to it. Bracing himself, he tore his gaze from the floor and directed it toward the bed.

Eliza was back.

Without warning, a scream erupted in Hank's throat, which clenched up, stifling it into a pitiful grunt. He swayed as the room began to swim, then his knees crumpled. He dropped to the floor, moaning out loud before plunging into a prattle of sobs, while Eliza lay silent and motionless on the bed.

Pull yourself together, Old Man. He squeezed his eyes shut, wringing out the tears, then pried his lids open wide. *This ain't really a surprise, is it?* He shook his head in response to the question, although if he was being honest, he'd admit he was secretly telling himself he'd discover a different outcome. Wishful thinking. *Foolishness was more like it.*

As he wiped his face dry, Hank noticed a scent that reminded him of meat that had started to rot. Opening his mouth for his next breath—the tip Ma had given him as a child—solved the problem.

After drawing in a deep inhale, he reached for the doorknob and pulled himself up to his feet, straining against the soreness in his muscles.

From the doorway, he leaned back and looked over his shoulder, checking to make sure nobody was lurking in the hallway. With no one in sight, Hank forced himself to turn Eliza's way. Her skin had taken on a darker shade of gray, cheeks more sunken, lips dry and pallid. The once-purple bruise on her cheek had turned charcoal-colored.

He pushed into the room, steeling himself for the floorboard creak, which sounded at the expected moment, yet still rattled his nerves. Two steps further, and he arrived bedside.

This time, Hank felt no need to touch Eliza's cadaverous face. But he did grab hold of her wrist, and when he lifted her arm, he immediately saw there was no lingering rigor mortis effect. He let go, and the arm dropped like a dead trout, her hand slapping the mattress with a dull thump.

His knees wobbled once again. Stiffening and locking them firmly, he shifted his gaze for a closer look at Eliza's face. She appeared as if she had two black eyes, but her sockets seemed almost hollow, causing her eyelids to droop inward. *Eyeballs like grapes withering into raisins,* a morbid inner voice pointed out.

Hank's mind whirled as he teetered on the brink of madness. "When will this end?" The question he cried shattered the silence of the room, but an eerie hush snuffed out the echoes of his voice, leaving the steady cadence of clock ticks as the only remaining sound.

When will this end?

Eliza's body lay utterly still, emphasizing the futility of asking. There was no one there to answer.

In this brutal ordeal, Hank Mitchell was all alone.

The screen door slammed shut behind Hank. He held up on the stoop, wringing his trembling hands, panting as he worked to recover his breath.

A minute later, with his head still spinning, he turned and stared at the door, lamenting how he couldn't lock it. But after Jimmy had lost their only key, Pop never bothered to replace the locks. Until now, Hank had never given it much thought; he rarely left the property, and when he did, there was nobody else around. *Should've barricaded the doors last night,* he admonished himself, although he had his doubts it would be so easy to seal this loathsome ritual out.

Hank pivoted around, sidestepped yesterday's heap of maggoty clothing, and positioned himself on the edge of the sandstone porch slab. He examined his surroundings suspiciously, watching for someone—*something*—who did not belong. Seeing nothing, he sucked in a long inhale and set off across the yard.

After passing the barn-side wildflower patch, Hank waded through the drift of fallen leaves behind the building. He detoured to the back fence of the family plot for a look, stopping beside the pile of rocks he'd deposited when he first buried Eliza, two days prior. The darkened hole of her open grave stood in stark contrast to the soil heaped beside it. With both fists squeezed around the fence posts, he scanned the ground but wasn't surprised to spot no traceable footprint evidence.

Choking up, Hank swallowed and pulled away from the grim scene, heading off for his escape destination.

The still-upright corn stood like armies of skeletons in formation, whispering to him as he crossed the field, the dry leaves fluttering in the warm breeze. Hank passed the scarecrow standing guard near the center, its black button eyes glaring across the valley.

A combine growled in the distance. The familiar sound of farm equipment comforted Hank. But when it occurred to him that his tenant farmer would be harvesting the corn he'd grown on the Mitchell property sometime in the next few weeks, Hank sighed. This meant yet another visitor since the equipment would be brought in past the barn.

By the time he reached the dam, Hank began feeling as if he had left an element of the insanity behind, confined within the farmhouse walls.

By instinct, he gave a cursory exam of the embankment, searching for signs of groundhogs burrowing, but saw nothing.

He followed the path to the side of the pond where the old elm with the tire swing once stood. It was on this tree where, while dating, Hank and Eliza had carved their initials inside a heart. Dutch elm disease claimed the stately tree in the 1980s, and a windstorm tore off most of its dead branches a few years later. Now, only the rotting skeleton of its trunk stood in its place, a sad reminder of what was lost. Their engraving had remained visible until the bark peeled off, erasing their declaration forever.

Nearby the remnants of the elm, Hank reclined on an enormous chunk of sandstone at the water's shore. A woolly bear caterpillar inched along the top of the rock, veering downward when it reached the edge, in search of a gap to burrow into for the winter. Hank studied the width of the rusty band in the middle of its length. Legend said the thickness of the brown band could predict how cold the coming winter will be: the wider the band, the milder the winter. Noting its unusually narrow width, Hank thought, *It's going to be a harsh one,* reminding him of what Nettie, the Amish produce stand girl, had said: "Winter is God's way of cleaning house."

Winter: when loneliness would catch up with him.

Yet this was a beautiful day. Beneath the cloudless, deep blue sky, the morning sun lit up the fall colors on the opposite side of the pond so vibrantly that the trees appeared to be on fire. The still water surface reflected the brilliant colors, doubling the effect.

There was something about the peacefulness of his surroundings which triggered Hank's sense of normalcy. If he had stayed in the house, he would have drowned in the misery of his plight. Instead, having put some distance between himself and the bad business at home, he began feeling as if he was breaking free from the anguish that had bedeviled him.

Two mallard ducks, a male and a female, paddled amongst fallen leaves floating on the surface at the far end, taking turns dunking their heads underwater. Their presence provided Hank with a welcome sign of life. The carefree creatures, oblivious to the awful situation he faced, combined with the picture-perfect weather and the autumn colors, making the bewildering events of the past couple of days seem distant...almost unreal.

Hank stared at the rotting elm tree trunk and thought of Eliza. With a sudden swell of grief, water pooled in his eyes. He wiped it away and sighed. "I miss you, dear." It occurred to him he was being deprived of the opportunity to mourn the loss of his wife. Rather, he was being forced to push his sorrow aside and deal with this cruel mystery. *It ain't fair.* But then he stopped himself. *Don't start with the self-pity, Old Man. Figure out what to do about it.*

The fiery colors across the pond spawned an outrageous thought: *Cremation.* The word stopped him cold...but still, as the idea clotted in his brain, he took it in and weighed it. A vile notion, yet he could not deny there was an element of logic to it: *If I cremate Eliza, she can't come back.*

Hank's mind began racing as he dwelled on the possibility. *Would that even work?* He didn't have an incinerator; only an open fire pit where he burned leaves and tree limbs. He had a few gallons of diesel fuel stored in the barn. Would that get the fire hot enough to do the job properly? Highly doubtful.

Just thinking about trying gave Hank a violent shudder.

Forget it, Old Man. There's no way.

Anyhow, you ain't that desperate.

...are you?

No.

"...not yet, at least." The words came out audibly but sounded like a whimper.

Straining to erase the revulsive concept from his mind, Hank kept his thoughts trained on finding a way to get to the bottom of the macabre matter. As he absently scratched a mosquito bite on his wrist, he pondered his other options, stumbling upon an idea that initially seemed so silly he almost dismissed it, then thought twice. The longer he contemplated it, the better it sounded.

"I reckon that just might work," he said out loud. He tried to spring up from the rock, eliciting screaming protests from his sore muscles. As he slumped back to the chunk of sandstone, he chuckled at his forgetfulness, then pushed himself up more gently.

Feeling for the first time in days a tendril of hope coiling around his heart, Hank Mitchell ventured home with a sense of purpose.

———————◄O►———————

When he arrived back at the farmhouse, Hank took the time to clean up the pile of clothing he'd left outside the rear door. He started with the pants, brushing them off and beating them against the sandstone slab to jar loose any still-lingering maggots. Something solid thwacked against the stone. Rummaging through the pockets, he came across the arrowhead he had found while burying Eliza, two days prior. He rubbed the smooth surface with his thumb for a moment before setting it aside, then turned his attention back to the task at hand.

Satisfied that he had ridden the cloth of all the remaining grubs, he gathered the clothing into a bundle and picked up the arrowhead. Inside, he slipped the artifact into the pocket of his winter coat, hung behind the door.

He tossed the clothes into the hamper at the foot of the cellar stairs, then went straight to the parlor. When Hank opened the closet door, he immediately spotted the vinyl bag he sought, on the floor, where it had sat untouched for at least a decade. He collected it by the handles and carried it to the kitchen, placing it on the table. The pouch was so dusty he had to wipe it down with a wet paper towel before unzipping it.

He reached in and hoisted out the massive VCR camera Eliza had splurged on for filming horse shows in the mid-80s. The bulky contraption was long-obsolete, but as far as Hank knew, it still worked.

He took the camcorder and the bag to the parlor and set about untangling the cords before connecting the device to the television. It didn't take long for him to determine the battery was dead and wouldn't even take a charge, but the unit came on when connected to AC power.

Relearning how to use the camera involved fiddling with an intimidating array of buttons. Just when he began to consider giving up on the whole idea, Hank managed to get the setup working, recording a test clip on an unopened tape he found in the bag.

"You did it, Old Man," Hank said, leaning back on the couch. "Well done." The horror of the last couple of days suddenly seemed to sink into the recesses of his mind...for the time being, at least. He knew it wouldn't last, though.

That was when Hank realized a light-headed feeling was taking hold. As he squeezed his fingers against his temples, his stomach growled. It dawned on him he had neither eaten nor had any caffeine yet, and the morning had mostly slipped away. He stood and turned toward the kitchen, then stalled and gazed up the stairway.

First, check on Eliza.

———◆◯◆———

As he shuffled down the hall to Eliza's doorway, Hank was met by the foul scent of decomposition. He suppressed the gag reflex and began breathing through his mouth.

From the bedroom entrance, he dragged his eyes over to Eliza. She lay undisturbed.

It's so cold.

As the words rang out in his mind, Hank's light-headedness worsened, and he soon found himself feeling short of breath.

It's so...dark.

Averting his gaze, he placed a hand on the doorjamb to brace against the swooning sensation.

When he gathered himself, he turned to leave, then hesitated. He sucked in a heavy inhale, held it, and then traversed the room, lifting the window all the way open before making a hasty exit.

Lunch consisted of a can of tuna, the last of an old bag of stale Shearer's potato chips (which he noted Brenda would have called "puh-too-tee" chips), and an apple from his own tree. He choked it all down with two mugs of coffee, figuring he needed the second to counteract the headache he had caused by delaying his morning dose of caffeine. After forcing down the last gulp, he headed upstairs to grab the .22 before collecting the recording gear.

Once the bag was repacked, he lifted the handles and carried it out the back door, toting the rifle in his other hand.

Upon edging into the barn, the feral tomcat hissed and darted into the gloom. Hank stifled a yelp. He sighed while collecting himself, propped the gun beside the door, and then wandered into the barn's interior, leaving the man door open to provide some light along his path.

When he flipped the light switch behind the workbench, the overhead fluorescent bulbs stuttered to life with a hum. A spider—the same one he had encountered two days prior, he soon realized—scurried into its pocket near the vise.

Hank set the bag on the end of the workbench and removed the camera. He fished around in the bottom of the pouch and located the portable tripod, which he unfolded. On a hook beside the workbench, a coiled extension cord hung. He plugged it into the nearby socket and unwound the cord as he maneuvered to the wall facing the graveyard.

After evaluating the window's height, he concluded the tripod could not reach high enough for the camcorder to capture the scene. He retrieved two sawhorses, set them up under the window, and bridged a strip of plywood over the top.

Within fifteen minutes, Hank had the gear mounted to the tripod on the plywood, and powered up. From his perch behind the setup on the stepladder, he played out his plan. He could get six hours of recording time by putting the camera on slow recording mode. If he activated it at eleven p.m., that would allow him to record until five a.m., which he reasoned would be enough time to capture whatever sick happenings were taking place overnight in the cemetery.

Just then, Hank heard gravel crunching, barely audible, the sound dampened within the barn's walls. He scrambled off the stepladder and hurried to the front, snatching the rifle before stepping outside. But by the time he had a view of the road, all he saw was a dust cloud the passing vehicle had left behind.

Could it have been the rusty white station wagon? It had passed by in the same direction. But there was no way to know, so he pushed it out of his mind, replaced the gun, and returned to the rear corner of the barn.

Back on the ladder, he trained the lens through the window. The viewfinder showed a blurry image, the filthy pane obscuring the camera's view. Wondering how long it had been since he'd last cleaned the glass, he returned to the floor, grabbed a rag from the workbench, and used it to wipe the inside surface.

After snapping on the heavy switch for the floodlight, he turned the camcorder on to RECORD and headed outside.

At the family plot's entrance, Hank peered upward and nodded. Even in the daytime, the floodlight, mounted on a gooseneck sconce near the top of the barn, shone brightly under its spun aluminum shade.

The gate wailed as he swung it open. Hank pulled off his cap and wandered into the graveyard, following inside the fence to where it ended, then along the barn's flank to its window. He reached up and scrubbed the grime off the outer surface of the pane using the cleaner side of the rag. The red LED glowed in the darkness, telling him the camera was recording.

He walked over to the open grave, turned around to face the red pinprick, posed for a moment, then made his way back to the barn.

After scaling the stepladder, Hank canceled the recording, rewound the tape, and pressed PLAY. He squinted into the tiny viewfinder screen and watched as he saw a blurry facsimile of himself wiping down the outside of the windowpane. The camcorder's autofocus shifted as he moved over to the grave, then resolved into a clear image of Hank Mitchell, posing graveside. He smiled with satisfaction at the crisp picture, canceled RECORD, and pressed REWIND.

As the tape rewound to the beginning, Hank climbed down from the ladder and stepped back to admire his handiwork. "Please don't fail me," he said out loud, reaching up to touch the camera as a measure of good luck.

———◆———

It was going on two o'clock when Hank reentered the house.

He poured himself a glass of water and found himself sipping it slowly. *Quit dawdling, Old Man.* He nodded and slugged down the last of it.

When he reached the top of the stairway, Hank could tell the odor had worsened, despite having opened the sash. *Or could the breeze coming through the window be spreading the smell?* With a shrug, he summoned his willpower and headed down the hallway, breathing through his mouth, which he was relieved to discover still took the edge off.

Without allowing himself to hesitate, Hank walked straight into the bedroom and over to the bed. He averted his eyes to avoid taking note of Eliza's deteriorating state while he cocooned her in the dirty quilt, cinching the free corners over her head.

When he lifted her, he immediately saw how Eliza had gone completely limp, almost as if her joints could now bend backward. It was a remarkable difference compared to two days prior when rigor mortis had turned her almost comically stiff. He wrapped his arms tightly around the bundle to make sure it didn't come undone. She seemed lighter yet, and it occurred to him that her body was probably drying out. He shook the thought away.

Carrying Eliza down the hall, Hank found it was no longer so easy ignoring the corpse stench, even with her wrapped inside the quilt. As he stepped down the last stair and turned the corner into the parlor, her foot whacked against the wall. *Be careful, Old Man.*

He crossed the lawn at a rapid clip, finding if he held her body low and moved quickly, he had mostly fresh air to breathe. But he felt winded by the time he reached the graveyard entrance, so he slowed his pace for the balance of the route.

When he arrived at her open grave, Hank lay Eliza on the mound of dirt beside the pit, then backed away to catch his breath. Once he felt ready, he stepped down into the grave and over to her torso, lifted her off the ground, and lowered her into the depths of her tomb.

This time, Hank did not bother smoothing the soiled bedcover shrouding, figuring there was little chance she'd be staying in the grave, anyway. He clawed his way out of the trench and proceeded to the barn to fetch the spade.

Upon his return, he promptly went to work covering Eliza's corpse with dirt. At first, his sore muscles objected, but the effort became bearable once he got warmed up. If there was a silver lining to reburying a body repeatedly, it was that the dirt got looser each time.

Feeling like he'd lost track of the days, he had to think it through. Yes, this *was* the third time he'd buried Eliza. Yesterday's burial—the second—had felt unceremonious compared to the first, but this iteration carried little feeling whatsoever. It seemed as if a part of him was shutting down. *Detachment...that's the word.*

As he threw one shovelful of dirt after another into the hole, he pondered what the videotape would divulge. Would it offer the answers he was seeking? If so, was there any way he could be satisfied with what it revealed?

Not a chance, if it turned out Eliza was crawling out herself.

Except, there was no indication this was what was happening. Even the way the sod had been stripped and the dirt had been piled beside the hole told him so.

Another question gnawed at the back of Hank's brain: if he figured out some person was behind this, what would he do about it? *After what you've done, it's not like you can call the sheriff.* He shook his head in exasperation.

When the pit was filled, he went to work on the sod layer, toiling on his hands and knees, arranging fragments like a living quilt. After patting the last piece into place, he pulled himself upright and picked up the spade to leave.

This time, he did not bother with any of the formalities. No tears. No thoughts of remembrance.

This time, Hank Mitchell was simply glad to be finished.

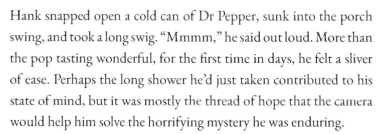

Hank snapped open a cold can of Dr Pepper, sunk into the porch swing, and took a long swig. "Mmmm," he said out loud. More than the pop tasting wonderful, for the first time in days, he felt a sliver of ease. Perhaps the long shower he'd just taken contributed to his state of mind, but it was mostly the thread of hope that the camera would help him solve the horrifying mystery he was enduring.

Wispy clouds with white, feathery strands were spreading across the western sky. As he studied them, he wondered if they portended the end of Indian Summer.

Within five minutes, he had drained his pop can. He reclined in the seat and used his legs to rock the swing. The gentle rocking lulled him like a baby in a cradle, and a few minutes later, he was fast asleep.

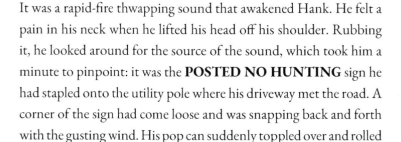

It was a rapid-fire thwapping sound that awakened Hank. He felt a pain in his neck when he lifted his head off his shoulder. Rubbing it, he looked around for the source of the sound, which took him a minute to pinpoint: it was the **POSTED NO HUNTING** sign he had stapled onto the utility pole where his driveway met the road. A corner of the sign had come loose and was snapping back and forth with the gusting wind. His pop can suddenly toppled over and rolled across the veranda.

Hank pulled himself out of the porch swing with a grunt. He fought against his sore muscles and the fresh pain in his neck to crouch down, retrieving the empty Dr Pepper can, so he wouldn't have to chase it into the bushes. He straightened upright, tilted his head back, and looked skyward. Thick clouds had crowded out the blue.

With a sigh, Hank went into the house, cut through the kitchen, where he tossed the can into the garbage, and continued through the back door. As he crossed the yard on the way to the barn, the wind blew so strong it almost ripped off his hat. He pressed it onto his head until he found refuge inside the barn.

Back in the work area, he scaled the stepladder, fired up the camera, and gave it a once-over. Convinced that everything looked okay, he turned off the power button and made his way to the workbench.

This time, when Hank approached, the resident spider clung to the middle of its web without bothering to hide. It was as if the spider was getting bolder, while Hank lost his aversion to it. He reached around the web, grabbed the Arrow heavy-duty stapler hanging on the pegboard, and headed to the exit, leaving the overhead lights on.

Back outside, Hank used a hand to secure his hat to his head. He followed the high-speed thwapping sound to the front yard, past the parked truck. When he waded through a drift of leaves that had accumulated along the side of the house, it evoked memories of a favorite boyhood pastime. But from the perspective of his current state, it all felt so distant.

Not wanting to have to replace the **NO HUNTING** sign, Hank went at it with the staple gun. Pop had tacked up the first postings eons ago. Even so, every couple of years, an unwelcomed hunter or two would trespass through the valley. So, while years of experience told Hank the signage was no cure-all, he had little doubt the situation would be even worse without prominent postings.

Half a dozen staples later, the loose corner of the sign was silenced and secured.

All at once, horse clopping arose. Hank groaned, realizing it was probably around five o'clock, and he would already be within sight of the bend in the road. It would be rude at the least to walk away. Worse yet, it might appear suspicious. Feeling like he was cornered, he removed his hat so it wouldn't blow away, turned around, and waited.

Levi Hostetler, in the lead buggy with a teenager beside him, tipped forward and waved, the narrow wheels bouncing on the crushed stone as the buggy approached.

Hank returned the wave while wondering if these men could be playing some role in his ordeal. As unlikely as it seemed, their presence *did* coincide with the diabolical turn of events.

When the horse closed in on the driveway, Levi steered over and pulled back on the reins, allowing the five lagging buggies to pass, each pair of men waving as they continued on their way.

"Hello, neighbor," Levi said.

"How've you been?" Hank asked.

"Purdy good," Levi said with his Amish accent, emphasizing the "purr" syllable. "This is my nephew, Enos. Enos, meet your future neighbor Hank."

Enos leaned forward, smiled, and tipped his tattered straw hat. A wind gust almost carried it away, but he caught it and pressed it into place while sliding back into the shelter of the carriage.

"Pleased to meet you, Enos."

Levi turned his eyes back to Hank. "I'm surprised I haven't been seeing you when we come through."

I've been on the wildest adventure, Hank imagined saying. Instead, he shrugged and looked up at the sky. "Seems like the weather's turning."

Levi peered upward and nodded. "I'd say so. Maybe we're finally going to get some fall weather. Or maybe we'll go straight into winter."

Hank gave a small chuckle. Hoping to wind down the small talk, he asked, "How's the construction coming along?"

"Purdy good. We should finish rough carpentry in two more days. We hope to be in by Christmas."

The wind gusted, whipping up a squall of leaves. Hank braced himself against the breeze and blocked his hair from his eyes using his free hand.

Levi slid back in his seat. "We'd better head home before the storm hits. My wife will have supper ready soon." He tipped his straw hat and shook the reins. His horse obeyed, and the buggy started rolling.

"Yeah." Hank cast a glance back at the farmhouse. "Mine too."

———◆———

Hank stared down at the shrouded figure nestled into the shadows of the grave.

Did she just turn her head?

A chattering sound made him jump. He glued his gaze on the cloaked head.

She is *moving.*

Her covered head trembled almost imperceptibly.

Like how she twitched during seizures.

The chatter, something awful, grew louder, more urgent.

Her teeth? Oh, God!

"I'm so cold," she uttered from the bottom of her tomb, her voice muffled by the shroud.

Part of Hank felt compelled to crawl down and hold her.

Part of him wanted to flee.

You can't. This is your *doing.*

The chatter swelled in volume.

Hank bolted upright. He looked around, disoriented, struggling to work out his dark surroundings. Light spilling into one side of the room revealed it to be the parlor. The chatter resumed—the window, rattling in its frame, it turned out.

Everything started coming back to him: after eating a chicken pot pie for supper, he had gone through the house and closed all the windows, then laid down on the daybed for a nap. He'd been dreaming.

Rain lashed against the nearby pane. He looked through it but saw nothing. Night had fallen. A quick stab of panic punched through his comatose state, breaking him free from the stupor. He hauled himself up from the couch, grimacing at his sore muscles.

After a stiff walk into the kitchen, he discovered it was going on midnight—well after the time he had planned to start the recording. "Damn it," he said out loud, hurriedly shrugging into his raincoat.

He yanked on his boots, flung the door open, and ventured out into the storm. The wind howled, tearing the hood from his head. He pulled it back on and tightened the drawstrings to hold it in place. As he sloshed over the saturated ground, a loose siding board on the barn clattered with another blast of wind.

Hank clenched his jaw as he drew in on the cemetery gate. Curtains of precipitation danced under the floodlight. With frigid spits of rain stinging his face, he cupped both hands to shield his eyes and blew out a shaking breath in relief when he saw that Eliza's grave remained covered.

After barging into the cover of the barn, Hank began shaking the water off his raincoat, but soon realized he was getting the rifle wet. He stepped clear and returned to the task while contemplating whether to barricade the house doors. But it was too late for that, wasn't it? Wouldn't that mess up his video recording plan? He decided this was a risk he could not take and would have to settle for bringing the gun into his bedroom.

The darkness folded in on him when he began his trek, drawn to the workbench light beacon spilling from the far reach of the interior.

As he closed in on the work area, a large moth fluttered into his face. Swatting at his head with both hands, he flinched backward, almost tumbling over the table saw. He righted himself and looked around. The workbench spider stared his way, like watching Hank's clown act from a bleacher seat in its web.

With a sigh, Hank Mitchell tramped over to the ladder, climbed two rungs, powered up the camera, and activated it to record at slow speed. He returned to the ground, but before turning to leave, he raised both hands toward the equipment and then crossed his fingers.

"Please don't fail me!"

CHAPTER 15

WINTER

OCTOBER 17, 2002

HANK WORKED TO BRING the clock into focus. He blinked, feeling like what he was seeing could not be right. It was after nine in the morning. *I never sleep in this late,* he thought, cringing as he rolled over. He lay there, dazed, vaguely aware that he needed to check something, but unable to put his finger on what.

Since he had not yet turned on the heat, the room had become so chilly his blankets had barely kept him warm. Outside, high gray clouds covered the sky. Although it was not raining, the clouds were enough to trigger his memory of the prior night's storm. When his mind stumbled upon the recollection of venturing out to start the camera in the barn, everything came back. He shook his head. *How could I forget?*

He rolled onto his side and spotted the gun propped against the wall, right where he had left it. But as he peeled off the covers and swung his legs over the edge of the bed, Hank did not question whether Eliza would be back in the house. The surprise would be if she wasn't.

When his bare feet came into contact with the cold wooden floor, he sucked in a breath through his teeth. Straightening upright, he let out a soft moan at the aches in his body. His shoulders and back felt the worst, the pain aggravated as he squirmed into his robe. When he set off for the bathroom, he discovered that even walking was a challenge.

Minutes later, Hank shuffled down the hall with nerves wound so tight he felt like a Jack-in-the-box on the verge of popping. *Be prepared,* he thought, and he gave a little nod.

Halfway to the bedroom, it was the noxious stink of roadkill on a hot summer day that told Hank Eliza's corpse was back. Undeterred, he held the sleeve of his robe against his face and pressed onward. As he stepped into the open doorway, he heard the muted buzz of flies echoing within the room.

When he lifted his line of sight to the bed, Hank found Eliza lying in the same spot as both days prior, but this time, begrimed with mud.

He looked away, assuring himself the recording would give him answers, and this abomination would soon be over. God, how he needed it all to end.

Unwilling to linger, he moved into the room, the vibration of flies growing in volume, the odor thickening with each pace forward. He held up behind the rocking chair, removed a handkerchief from his robe pocket, and covered his face with it. *Breathe through your mouth,* he reminded himself, although he already knew that old trick wouldn't be enough anymore.

When he took another step, the floor creaked. The quilt was caked in drying mud, Eliza's face and hair checkered in smears. Her skin color had darkened to a sickening gray, the facial bruise no longer even visible.

Although Hank desperately wanted to look away, part of him felt obligated to look closer. Unable to withstand the compulsion, he stepped forward and leaned in. Eliza's neck, cheeks, and eyes had bloated, putrefaction distorting her face into a gruesome, swollen appearance, puffiness stretching her lips thin. Cocked slightly open, her mouth exposed the shriveled tip of her tongue, the color of spoiled liver, protruding out from a layer of brown foam seeping up from her throat.

The muted hum of flies resumed, and Hank's distress ratcheted up with the realization of where they were hiding. He reached out to the mattress with his free hand and shook it. "Get out of there, bastards!"

The flies momentarily went quiet, leaving the ticking clock as the only sound in the room. Since the flies remained out of sight, Hank considered prying open her mouth to chase them out but promptly swept aside the repulsive notion.

His heart wrenched into a painful knot. How could this be his beloved wife? She'd been so beautiful. Now, all he could feel was revulsion.

The flies resumed buzzing, giving Eliza a ghoulish death voice.

With a long groan, Hank turned away from the ghastly sight, then fled the room as fast as his aching legs could carry him.

When he burst out the back door of the farmhouse, Hank immediately regretted he hadn't taken time to put on clothes. He had grabbed the rifle and slipped into his boots, but was so anxious to escape he hadn't even put a jacket on over his pajamas and bathrobe. With no sunshine breaking through the clouds to warm the air, a sharp northerly breeze cut right through to his skin.

His breath came in raw, ragged gasps as he huffed past the grind-stone-capped well on his way to the barn. When he arrived, he bent forward to read the rusting old thermometer sign mounted beside the man door (**TIME for a new Ford** declared across the top). The mercury showed 44°F—a more than 25-degree temperature drop compared to recent days. *So much for the warm spell.*

Feeling as though the cold was flushing the fog out of his head, Hank turned and surveyed his surroundings. The winds had stripped many of the colorful leaves from their trees, leaving some branches virtually bare. As they swayed in the breeze, the exposed limbs looked like black skeletal fingers reaching out, grabbing...

Down the country road, a patch of Shirley's decaying farmhouse peeked out through the trees that had grown around it, unmasked for the first time since spring. The Ghoul House's sickly gray siding reminded Hank of the color of Eliza's skin. With a hard swallow, he wiped the leaking corners of his eyes and looked away.

He pulled open the door, stepped inside, and set the gun against the wall beside the entranceway. Normally, the musty scent of the barn stirred up comforting sentiments, but at this moment, it did little to soothe Hank's agitation.

Back in the workshop, he flipped on the overhead light switch. The area lit up, but the spider stood its ground in the middle of the web, eyeing Hank intently, like looking into his soul. Hank shivered and backed away.

After scaling the stepladder, he powered up the camera and pressed the eject button with trembling hands. Gears churned, and the machine popped open. Hank drew in a deep shuddering breath, slid out the tape, and climbed down to head back to the house.

---◄○►---

Hank's teeth chattered as he pushed the tape into the VHS player under the television. *Turn the heat on, Old Man,* he told himself, but then he responded aloud, "No, it can wait."

When he pressed the REWIND button, the machine whirred up to speed. While he waited for what seemed to take forever, Hank's mind rifled through the possibilities of what the video might reveal. Either Eliza herself was clawing her way out of the grave, or someone had to be digging her up. *Or some*thing.

The machine gave a loud click when the tape reached the beginning, causing Hank to flinch. He pressed PLAY with his quivering thumb and slid back into his seat, his heart pounding unnaturally fast. *And now, the moment of truth.*

An image appeared on the tube. Hank leaned forward. The recorded picture, dark and murky, shimmered and shifted on the screen. Staring at it, he squinted, working to sort out what he was seeing. He soon realized that water was sheeting down the outside of the window, warping the scene. Hank suddenly felt light-headed. Was the entire recording distorted beyond recognition?

Maybe not, he reassured himself. Perhaps the problem was that the camera had nothing to focus on, he reasoned. *Maybe it'll clear up when something happens.*

After watching the writhing picture for a minute, Hank pressed the FAST-FORWARD button. The tiny motors droned at high speed while snowy bands rolled from the bottom of the tube to the top, and shadows danced in rapid movements.

A long time passed without the recording revealing anything recognizable, and Hank's hope that the video would provide any clues on the mystery began to dwindle. A few minutes later, with still no change, another painful thought entered his mind: maybe whatever happened had taken place after the tape's six-hour limit. Hank felt his face growing hot, but he told himself to be patient.

The shadows continued to shimmy haphazardly until, suddenly, an indistinct figure appeared, seemingly from out of nowhere. The hairs stood up on the back of Hank's neck. He lunged for the machine and canceled the fast-forward, returning the tape playback to normal speed. Taking a kneeling position in front of the television, his breathing ceased to be an involuntary action. He commanded his lungs to do their job and fought to calm himself down as he studied the screen.

Poor lighting and the optical distortion from the sheeting water running down the outside surface of the window left everything dark and blurred. The obscured silhouette hovered over Eliza's grave, the grainy image oscillating between bad and worse while the camera's autofocus hunted for a target but failed to lock onto it.

After a spell, the figure began chiseling into the ground, using what must have been a shovel. "God damn you!" Hank spat the words at the tube. "How dare you?"

Overwhelmed with the newfound understanding that someone was doing this heinous thing to Eliza, all the while tormenting him while he slept, Hank desperately wished once again he could lock the house's doors.

He stared at the shadow, searching for distinguishable features as the gravedigger worked. But this proved to be as futile as grabbing a handful of smoke. Appearing as little more than a gauzy, colorless outline, Hank simply could not determine who this might be—or even whether it was a man or a woman.

After a while, he began fast-forwarding through the digging, but he returned to regular speed when the shadow crouched out of view in the grave. The figure rose, clutching the bundled corpse, and then climbed out of the hole, picked up the spade, and slipped out of the frame.

Leaning back against the couch, a sinking feeling formed in Hank's gut. He held his gaze on the television but saw nothing. After an extended span without any activity, he resumed the fast-forward, holding a numb stare while the machine hummed at high speed, with seconds amassing into minutes.

Eventually, the machine emitted a disheartening audible click when the tape reached its end, and as the videotape player began to automatically rewind, the TV screen filled with snow.

——◦○◦——

Unable to face what lay upstairs, Hank needed to escape the house. Clothed and bundled up in his winter coat, he went out to the front veranda to force down his coffee and a strawberry Pop-Tart he'd heated in the toaster. Pop-Tarts had always been one of Eliza's guilty pleasures. They were too dry for Hank's taste, but he was running low on food choices, and, well...Eliza's snacking days were over.

Swaying weakly on the porch swing, he stared into the distance at nothing, feeling so broken and defeated he couldn't even cry. The dash of hope he'd tasted the day prior had turned sour. *Still don't know what's going on.* There had been no sense in reviewing the video. The distortion from the rain completely obscured the gravedigger's identity. He began chastising himself for not having foreseen this possibility.

As Hank thought about it further, it dawned on him that his main concern had been trying to determine how Eliza's body had been getting out of the grave and into the house. At least the video answered this riddle in a general sense. He now knew someone—*or some*thing—was digging her up. *Well, that's a start, I reckon.* After all, Eliza clawing out on her own power was the worst-case scenario, right? What would he have done then?

That *was* something, he had to admit. But who—*or what*—remained the most caustic mystery imaginable. And then there was the question of why. Why would someone do this? What did they want?

Hank wiped the strawberry filling from his lips onto his sleeve and took the last gulp of the now-cold coffee. A wind gust whipped a squall of dead leaves from the mostly bare apple tree, some of which made their way onto the porch, where they vortexed into the center, coming to rest near his feet.

The idea of calling the sheriff crossed briefly through Hank's mind. The concept offered a certain appeal: someone else would share the burden of solving this grim puzzle. But he promptly dismissed the notion, knowing that if the law got involved now, he would be the first to land in jail.

Hank wondered if perhaps he hadn't thought things through well enough in the first place. What if he had reported Eliza's death rather than keeping it a secret? How much risk would there really have been of the authorities suspecting foul play? Since she had been terminally ill, would they have even done toxicology tests? Hank shook his head and sighed. *The horse has left the barn.* Anyway, how could he have anticipated the demonic occurrences that followed?

Hank pushed himself out of the swing, grunting as he straightened his back, then wandered across the veranda. He placed the empty John Deere mug on the railing and canted out over it, gazing sightlessly across the valley.

The thought of a cigarette popped in his head once again, and this time, he even went as far as to momentarily deliberate venturing up to the drive-through liquor store on the edge of Clarkton to pick up a pack of Camels. *Forget it, Old Man. You might run into someone you know. Ain't no good can come from that.*

When he slid his hands into his jacket pockets to warm his cold fingers, Hank came upon the arrowhead. He pulled it out and studied it. The artifact reminded him that, considering human history's long passage, his suffering was inconsequential. *But still, it matters to me.* Fair enough, he reasoned, but the presence of the arrowhead could at least help him keep things in perspective. *And maybe, if you keep your wits about you, you can find a way through this nightmare.*

He steered his thoughts back to the mystery. In a sense, knowing that someone was the perpetrator of this gruesome routine reassured him, because this meant there was a way to end it. Except, his skin crawled at the thought that someone was coming into the house while he slept.

Who could it be? He thumbed through the suspects. Pastor Lionel Burns. The rusty white station wagon driver. The multitude of Amishmen working down the road.

But what if it was someone else entirely?

If only the camera had captured a full view of the figure's face! As he lamented the dark and distorted recorded image, an idea popped into Hank's mind: he could set up the camcorder in Eliza's bedroom. *Of course. That's the solution!* He shook his head, questioning why he hadn't thought of this simple approach to begin with.

If he left the bedroom light on, there would be plenty of light for the camera, and no distortion because of glass or rainwater. Moreover, the gravedigger would come close enough to the recording equipment when they carried Eliza's body into her room that a full view of their face would be virtually assured.

"That's the answer," he declared. Riding a fresh wave of something like hope, Hank picked up the empty mug and made for the door.

Like it or not, the time had come for yet another burial.

———◆◇◆———

Even before he had reached the midpoint of the hallway, Hank was fighting to ignore the odor of rot emanating from the bedroom. He considered retreating to fetch his respirator, but dismissed the idea, feeling like it would somehow be an insult to Eliza.

After drawing in a sharp breath, he walked straight into the room without lingering, taking long strides to hasten his arrival at Eliza's bedside. Although she remained still, the muffled sound of buzzing flies persisted, a droning sound worming its way into his skull.

He stood over her and hesitated for a few seconds, her disfigured face grabbing and holding his attention, pulling him into some sort of morbid curiosity trance.

He clenched his eyelids shut, mustering the strength to snap free from whatever had taken hold of him. When he reopened his eyes, he went to work, moving swiftly to cover her swollen features. The mud that coated the quilt had hardened to a crust, cracking and falling off in chunks as he wrapped it around her. He paused to gasp in another breath, stifling the gag reflex the foul air triggered.

When he lifted Eliza's decaying body, the flies ceased buzzing.

As he carried her down the stairs, the idea of cremating Eliza pounced back into Hank's head. Cremation would put an end to the horrifying daily chore he was being forced to endure, a routine that was becoming increasingly dreadful with each passing day. There was nothing absurd about the concept. No, as twisted as it was, there was a certain logic to it. It would be an unspeakable act, though, too horrific to even contemplate, so he tossed the vile notion aside while he slipped his feet into his boots at the back door.

Hank gritted his teeth, steeling for the screech of the hinges as he pushed open the iron gate. He lugged his grisly load inside the cemetery, groaning at the sight of the saturated mud pile, eroded by countless washout rivulets that had erased all footprint evidence.

When he arrived at the foot of the open grave, he halted. Standing rainwater filled the bottom. Unable to tell how deep it was, he told himself it was only a couple of inches.

In the absence of jostling movements, the muted buzzing resumed. *Quit dawdling, Old Man.*

The flies went silent when he stepped into the grave, but a split second later, he felt the ground give way under his heels. He promptly lost his footing altogether, sliding down the muddy slope, and landing with a soggy thump on his rear end. Eliza bounced on his lap.

"Sorry." The word left him like an involuntary reflex, but he didn't allow himself to feel foolish for it. He righted himself and stepped all the way into the water, which he immediately discovered was deeper than his boots. Icy water rushed in, swamping his feet.

He set his jaw, waded forward several steps, bent over, and lowered Eliza's body to the water's surface. He vacillated for a spell, then released her. The quilt began bubbling as her corpse sank. Hank groaned at the sight of it. Anxious to cover her, he slithered out of the muddy hole, poured the water out of his boots, and headed for the barn to retrieve the shovel.

When he returned, he faltered. He stood at the foot of the hole, trying not to look at the half-submerged cadaver below, feeling paralysis set in. Fully prepared to shrug off his body aches, it was the totality of the situation, the wrongness of it all, which gave him pause. This would be his fourth attempt to bury Eliza. How had it come to this? Could anyone have ever imagined such a nightmare? *Never mind that, Old Man. Get on with it.*

He complied, but when he stuck the spade into the mound of mud, he quickly realized how much harder it would be to move the wet, densely packed dirt, compared to the previous couple of days, when the fill had been loose and dry. He momentarily questioned whether he should use the backhoe for the task, but decided against it, lest anyone come through and witness the suspicious activity. *Quit dawdling,* he repeated to himself.

As he began filling the hole, a thought formed in his head: if he removed a section of the fencing, he could park the tractor over the grave, blocking access to whoever was digging Eliza up. He concluded this idea might be something to consider, but not tonight. He could not interfere with Plan A, the camera in the bedroom.

Each clump of muck he threw splashed in the grave-tub until the water—and Eliza's corpse—had been covered. He kept at it without any breaks and had the trough filled in little more than an hour. This time, he decided to forego the sod layer, not seeing the point, considering it would soon all be undone.

Leaning against Jimmy's headstone, Hank removed his boots one at a time, dumped a little more water from each, and wrung out his socks. After putting them back on, he brushed himself off and picked up the shovel to return it to the barn.

When he was just about to enter the barn, he heard the distant sound of a car, sending his stomach into a somersault. He hopped over the man door's threshold and pulled the door closed behind him, then peeked out to see who was passing through.

Sure enough, it was the same wretched rusty white station wagon.

Hank glared at the vehicle as it slowed down near his home, disappeared from view as it passed, then reemerged on the other side. It coasted onward, but the brake lights lit up as it approached Shirley Gould's house. This time, the car halted, then nudged into the roadside weeds, where it parked.

Hank felt heat flaring on his face as he watched the car door pop open. A scarecrow of an old man wearing long white hair tilted out and looked his way. But the intruder was nobody Hank recognized. He clambered out of the car, keeping one hand on the door, staring in the direction of the Mitchell homestead.

"You son of a bitch," Hank growled, reaching for his .22.

When he looked back out again, the man was easing his door closed without a slam. The intruder labored across the road into what was left of Shirley's driveway, then vanished behind the overgrowth.

With bared teeth, Hank set off on a beeline toward the pond, determined to sneak up on his foe.

Fueled by rage, Hank made good time, despite his sore muscles slowing him down and his feet squishing inside the soggy boots with every step. Panting, he crossed paths with the genuine scarecrow, who kept his gaze fixed across the valley.

As he came upon the dam, he spotted a groundhog at the opposite end. Both man and critter froze at the same instant and stared each other down. On instinct, Hank shifted his hold on the rifle and prepared to aim, then paused to give it some thought. Surely, the sound of a gunshot would scare off the human intruder before Hank had a chance to confront him. When Hank sighed and continued on his way, the creature bounded down the embankment, disappearing into the brush.

At the end of the dam, Hank hastened into the trail that snaked alongside the creek, leading to the opening behind Shirley Gould's farmhouse. He held up where the trail reached the clearing to scan Ghoul House and its surroundings. The white station wagon was visible in the distance, but there was no sign of the old man.

Hank barreled down the slope to where the trail ran along the collapsed side of the old dwelling. He slowed his pace when he arrived at the back corner of the structure, watching on high alert for the stranger. As he approached the front of the house, he drew in closer to the ruins, his shoulder brushing against the tattered clapboards.

The wind blew, rattling a loose section of the crumpled tin roof above. The collapsed upper floor of the structure groaned, perhaps settling a little under the strain.

Hank stopped just short of the front, wiped his free hand on the driest patch of his pants, transferred the gun to the other, and did the same with the opposite palm. Grasping the rifle in two drier hands with his right positioned near the trigger guard, he advanced one more pace, pitched forward, and peered around the house. Still nothing.

He rounded into the front and began edging toward the opposite end of the dwelling. As he crept past the gaping hole that had once been the front door, he snuck a glance inside, despite knowing there could be nobody there, since the floor had given way long ago. Shadows crowded the wrecked interior, but there was no sign of life.

A few steps further, Hank came across a strip of reddish-brown fur, a few rib bones, and one sun-bleached antler. He gave a somber nod as he sidestepped the remnants of the buck's carcass.

Leaning into the house for cover, he tiptoed up to the opposite corner. When he peeked around, Hank saw the skeletal old man picking his way through the weeds, heading toward...the Gould family graveyard?

With clenched teeth, Hank stepped out, following the intruder's path, but keeping a fixed distance behind. Languishing overgrowth rustled in the brisk breeze, drowning out Hank's footfalls and the hushed squooshing noises inside his boots.

Soon, the rickety man arrived at the cemetery. With trembling hands and a pounding pulse, Hank continued forward, narrowing the gap between them, closing in to finish the ambush. When a twig cracked under one step, the man's head snapped around.

Hank halted in his tracks, leveled the gun, and pointed it at his adversary.

With eyes the size of turnips, the intruder threw up his hands. "Don't shoot!"

Hank glowered at the man with the gun aimed, his finger brushed against the trigger. If Hank had to guess, the stranger was well over eighty—probably every bit of ten years his senior. "What do you want?"

"I'm sorry," the old man said, raising his hands further.

"What do you want?" Hank snarled, drawing in closer. They were less than twenty feet apart by now. All the anger Hank had been holding inside over the past several days erupted, and it was all he could do to keep from squeezing the trigger.

"Please!" The bastard dropped to his knees. "I don't mean no harm."

"Why are you here?"

The old man turned his head toward the tiny family plot and back to Hank, then croaked, "To apologize."

Hank squinted and pulled back his head. "To who?"

The intruder trembled, then tossed his head backward, gesturing toward the Gould family graveyard. "The old dame who was buried there."

Hank took a step forward and lined up the sights. "Apologize for what?"

The stranger lowered his chin and broke into tears. Within seconds, he covered his face with his hands.

"For *what?*" Hank demanded, drawing in.

"Me and my brother, we dug her up." The pitiful old man began to bawl, and a few moments later he blubbered, "He made me. I was just a stupid kid."

When the old man yanked open the station wagon door, its hinges creaked, sending an explosion of crows into flight from the nearby creek-side stand of trees. Stationed on the other side of the road with his back to Shirley Gould's house, Hank turned his eyes skyward to watch the aerial stampede.

Still holding the gun in both hands, he no longer pointed it at the intruder. After the crows scattered, he said, "Roll down your window before you get in. And keep your hands where I can see them."

The man complied, cranking down the glass without asking why. He slid in and shut the groaning door. With his left hand resting on the steering wheel, he looked straight ahead while turning the ignition. The tired old clunker's engine cranked away in vain for a span before eventually firing. He shifted into drive and then placed his right hand on the steering wheel. As he began pulling out of the weeds, Hank stopped him. "Wait."

The old man braked, then put the gearshift back into park.

"What did you do with her bones?"

The intruder dropped his head, lowering his gaze down in the direction of his lap. The idling car rumbled for half a minute while he worked up his response. "I dumped them in Salem Lake."

Hank cocked his head. "Why'd you do that?"

"My brother got into big trouble. Not long after we dug her up, he was charged with murder."

"Murder?"

"Arson. Four people died."

Hank considered this. "The Cutler family?"

The old man nodded and turned to face Hank for the first time since entering the car. "He had some stupid grudge against the father."

Big Homer County news at the time, Hank remembered the tragic case well. "The couple and their two kids burned to death." He paused, rubbing his chin in reverie. "One...was an infant."

The old man nodded again, solemnly. "They tried my brother as an adult. Gave him the electric chair in 1945. I'd be the first to say he deserved it."

Neither spoke for a stretch, until Hank eventually asked, "Why'd you put Shirley's bones in the lake?"

"My brother stashed them in a canvas duffel bag, hidden inside our woodshed. After he got arrested, I started to worry the Sheriff would come snooping around. If they found those bones, I'd have been in a real pickle. So, one night I took the sack to the dam, added a good-sized rock, and tossed it in the lake."

"Geez," Hank said, shaking his head. "They never found the bones?"

The old man shrugged. "Probably still there, I reckon. I never told a soul...until now. I shoved off after that. Hopped a train and went out west. Got a clean start in California and lived right. When my wife died last month, I drove back. I always wanted to make amends."

"Why'd you dig her up in the first place?"

"It wasn't my idea. My brother heard all sorts of stories. Shirley was a ghost, or a witch, or some such thing. He'd been getting hung up on witchcraft, satanism...crazy stuff like that. Kept talking about how digging her up would give us powers. What baloney. All I got out of it was guilt that stuck with me for life. Dead bodies should be left in the ground."

Hank glanced down the road at his farmhouse and repeated the words in his head: *Dead bodies should be left in the ground.* He muttered under his breath, "What a concept."

"What was that?"

"Never mind."

The old man sniffed and wiped his face with both hands. "For a while, I thought my brother was just talking. Then, one night, he wakes me up after midnight, tells me it's time. We drove down from the other side of Clarkton and parked up the road." He pointed through his windshield in the direction of the bend. "Wasn't hard. There was no vault—no coffin, even. Seems she hadn't been embalmed either, since all we found was bones and scraps of cloth. She was buried like a pauper."

The men fell silent as that notion sunk in. When a sharp breeze blew, Hank secured his hat to his head.

The intruder sniffed again. "Anyway, I'm really sorry to bother you."

Hank furrowed his brow. "No big deal."

"...and thanks for giving me a chance to say my piece to the old dame. I said it on the Salem Lake dam, but that ain't enough. I had to say it here, too."

Hank nodded.

"I tried to come by each of the last three days, but chickened out each time." He pointed his thumb over his shoulder at Hank's house. "Saw your truck, so I knew someone was home. Kept worrying one of you folks might see me."

Hank stepped back off the gravel, playing back the words.

...one of you folks...

The old man turned the wheel and began pulling out of the weeds, then stopped once again. "Can we..." He chewed on his lower lip for a few seconds. "...keep this between us?"

Hank scratched the back of his neck, then lifted the gun over his shoulder. "So long as you're done here."

The visitor nodded emphatically. "Thanks. I'll be hitting the highway and heading west from here." He faltered for a spell, then looked Hank in the eye. "You know, I ain't proud of what I done." He cast his gaze down, his face resolving into a miserable expression of shame.

Hank raised his eyebrows. "No, I reckon you ain't."

The old man turned to face the windshield, let off the brake, and the car began to roll.

Half a minute later, the rusty white station wagon—with a California license plate tacked on the rear bumper—drove off and disappeared around the bend, leaving behind a cloud of dust mingled with the scent of burned oil.

The noxious odor of rot overwhelmed Hank the moment he entered the front door. Eliza was gone from the house, but her fetid scent had spread down to the lower level, clinging to the interior. After propping the rifle beside the front door, he covered his nose with his handkerchief and went through the house, opening each of the windows that could still be raised (about half).

Within fifteen minutes, the air had cleared considerably. *Or maybe you're getting used to it?* He shrugged, then went back through the house, lowering the sashes, except for the one in Eliza's room, where the rank smell lingered thickest. He shut the bedroom door.

Still wearing his jacket, he checked the thermostat. "56 degrees?" He shook his head. "Seems even colder than that." He decided he'd close Eliza's bedroom window by dark, then fire up the furnace.

In the kitchen, he combed through the freezer, pulling out a Salisbury Steak TV dinner. Although it was not yet even four o'clock and he had zero appetite, Hank knew he needed to eat. At least turning on the oven would warm up the immediate area, he figured.

As he huddled over the stove's heat while waiting for his supper, the gears in his mind cranked away. The rusty white station wagon had been one of his prime suspects. It was a strange turn of events, but there was no doubt the old man was being forthcoming about everything. So, the mystery of what had happened to Shirley Gould's grave was finally solved, with no zombie element in the explanation. Meanwhile, the driver of that car was no longer a possible culprit behind Eliza's removal from the grave, so Hank's bewilderment had only deepened.

The appliance timer buzzed, jarring Hank out of his thoughts.

He donned the oven mitt and retrieved the foil tray. When he peeled it open, steam poured out from inside, but the smell of it turned his stomach.

He dumped what was left in the milk jug into a glass, filling it only halfway. *Going to need to make a grocery run before long,* he thought as he sat down to eat, then sighed. It would have to be a trip to the tiny Amish store nestled in the Duffey Valley, where there was virtually no risk of running into someone he knew. Since the Amish shops don't sell cigarettes, this would help him resist the temptation of his vice.

After finishing a fraction of the supper, Hank felt overcome with exhaustion. Still so chilled he felt like the cold had penetrated the marrow of his bones, he stretched out on the daybed wearing his jacket, bundling himself under two blankets.

As he listened to the sound of the departing Amish buggies passing the house, he told himself, *Thankfully, you got the burial done early today,* and soon, fatigue overtook him.

⬤

It was dark when Hank awakened.

No nightmares during this nap, he noted with relief as he rubbed the sleep from his eyes. Lacking the energy to get up, and not wanting to come out from under the blankets, he remained on the daybed, dozing in and out for a while longer.

When he reawakened for good, he pushed himself upright, groaning from the soreness. He flipped on the light switch and discovered it was almost nine o'clock, making this the longest nap he'd ever remembered having.

After compelling himself to eat more of the supper, Hank went out the back door, holding up on the stoop to survey his surroundings.

The sky had cleared. A rising gibbous moon hung under the Milky Way. The temperature had dropped further with nightfall, and each breath sent a vapor plume into the chilly air. *Feels like Halloween.*

The cemetery glowed under the barn-mounted floodlight, still burning from the night prior. Eliza's grave lay undisturbed. *Thank goodness. For now, at least.* Hank stepped off into the grass, and with frost crunching underfoot, made for the barn to retrieve the recording gear.

Fortunately, he had left the workbench overhead lamp on, lighting his interior path. Back in the work area, he toggled the outside floodlight off, figuring there was no sense in making the miscreant's task any easier.

The spider stood guard as he unhooked the camera and disassembled the tripod, arranging both in the vinyl pouch. After rolling up the extension cord, he grasped the handles and lifted the bag. "Good night," he said to the onlooking arachnid, then headed back to the house.

Inside, Hank took a detour into the cellar, where he lit the furnace pilot light. In the parlor, he checked the thermostat, which showed the temperature had dropped further, now reading 52 degrees. He turned the dial, lining up the arrow with 65.

A queasy feeling took hold in his gut as he proceeded down the hallway toward the closed door of Eliza's room. He held his breath, pushed the door open, and switched on the light. Unable to stop himself, he looked at the bed...empty, as it should be. *For now.*

As he breathed through his mouth, he was relieved to discover that enough of the odor had cleared to tolerate it. He placed the vinyl bag on the foot of the bed and lowered the open sash.

With the gear in tow, he rounded across to the opposite side of the bed, pulled open the closet door, and nodded. The camera could be positioned between the hanging clothes—still Brenda's, all these years later. He went to work unfolding the tripod and stringing the extension cord behind the bed's headboard, hiding it from view.

Setting up the recording equipment drove home the unsettling notion that someone would be coming into the house while he slept down the hall. *Except, it seems this character ain't too interested in you, Old Man.* In any case, barricading the doors was not an option on this night.

Upon powering up the camcorder, he tunneled in behind the clothing, adjusting the angle so the viewfinder was trained on the bedroom doorway.

After convincing himself the equipment was ready to go, Hank left it behind to chase away the last of his chill with a hot shower.

Clean, warm, and dressed in his pajamas, he returned to Eliza's room. He leaned into the closet, pressed RECORD on the camera, and nodded when the LED lit up and the motors whirred into action.

Withdrawing from the closet, he nudged the hanging clothes inward to cloister the equipment, then lifted one arm of the nearest blouse and draped it over the camera, covering the glowing LED. With both hands raised, fingers crossed, he said, "Please don't fail me."

Hank left the bedroom light on, made one last trip downstairs to collect the gun, and then headed for bed, closing his door behind him.

CHAPTER 16

REVELATION

OCTOBER 18, 2002

H ANK MITCHELL AWOKE AT almost 9:30 the next morning. *Geez, I'm sleeping in later every day,* he thought, wincing at the soreness in his muscles as he rolled over.

He struggled to recollect the details of what had happened the day prior. With the days blurring together, it was becoming difficult to keep the course of events straight. The radiator clicked and creaked, reminding him how he'd turned on the heat. Then he recalled the camera he had set up in Eliza's room. *Oh, yeah—round two.*

As he folded himself upright, he squeezed his eyes shut against the sharp pain that shot down his spine and into his legs. With several blinks, he thought, *This is worse than just sore muscles.*

Knowing he had business to tend to, Hank gutted through the physical hurt, gingerly swinging his legs over the side of the bed, moaning under his breath as he moved.

After resting for a minute, he planted his feet on the floor and gritted his teeth against the discomfort while slowly straightening his back until he was standing erect. Soon, he found that even stretching into his robe and sliding his feet into his slippers was no effortless task. He paused to recover, steadying himself by placing his hand on the dresser.

His temples throbbed as he struggled to shake the dazed feeling from his head. Fresh cigarette cravings crept back into the forefront of his thoughts. When he had been a regular smoker, Hank remembered feeling a cigarette could clear his mind—although he was never certain it really worked that way, and the first smoke of the day seemed particularly rejuvenating. He sighed and shook the craving aside.

Unable to manage anything more than baby steps, Hank shuffled across the floor. When he pulled on his bedroom doorknob, he noticed it was not latched completely closed. *Didn't I shut it all the way?* He looked back at the rifle, which remained beside his bed, just as he had left it.

The putrid stench of rot hit him when he entered the hall, erasing any sliver of doubt that Eliza was back. *Like a vile, endless loop,* he thought. *It's a curse.* Worse yet, it was nearly impossible to imagine a happy outcome to all this. While praying that the camera's recording would provide him some form of closure, he held the handkerchief over his face, breathed through his mouth, and compelled himself down the corridor.

As he stepped into Eliza's doorway, he attempted to hold his breath, but a small, inadvertent gulp of noxious air was all it took. His stomach reflex took over, spewing vomit across the floor, the unexpected hurl projecting his belly's contents halfway to the foot of the bed.

Hank leaned against the doorjamb, wiping bile from his lips with the hankie, fighting against the urge to flee. Without warning, his gut lurched again, the dry heave causing an excruciating stab of pain that bolted down his back and legs.

While he struggled to recover from the pain and to calm his stomach despite the sickening odor, he counted to ten. He heard Ma whisper, "Breathe through your mouth, Hank," and he nodded. It helped a bit, but the stink was so strong he could practically taste it.

When he finally felt capable of standing upright again, Hank shambled toward the bed, unable to tear his gaze from Eliza's corpse as he drew in. Mud was smeared all over her; the quilt and her hair and bedclothes remained wet from the standing water she had been submerged in. Her mottled skin had darkened to a greenish charcoal color. With distended cheeks and neck pulling her face taut, her skin stretched so thin it appeared to be on the verge of splitting. Her eyeballs were bloated beyond the reach of her eyelids, exposing hideous bands of the bulging orbs. Appearing like they might pop at any moment, her cadaver pupils glowered at the ceiling.

Enlarged nostrils revealed two gaping nasal passages from which the disgusting brown foam bubbled out. A couple of maggots crawled along the inside of her lips, and others writhed from within the coffee froth that had percolated up from the esophagus to fill her oral cavity. When he came to the distressing conclusion that Eliza's body was probably now full of maggots—the flies had surely laid eggs inside her mouth—Hank promptly threw up again, this time, on the floor beside the nightstand.

When he finished retching, he shuffled back to his own bedroom to collect himself and settle his stomach. Except, he soon realized he had not retrieved the VCR tape, so he would have to return.

Hank leaned on the edge of his bed and wrestled with his psyche, focusing on the strangled gasp of hope that the video would hold some answers.

Ready for another try, Old Man? Blinking away his doubts, he pushed himself onto his feet. He picked a fresh handkerchief from the stack on top of his dresser, unfolded it, and covered his face. As he stepped into the hallway once again, he decided he'd go straight for the video camera.

When he turned into Eliza's bedroom, he held his breath and hustled toward the closet, sidestepping the slop of retch while avoiding looking her way. Upon retrieving the videotape, he fled the room as fast as his stiff, sore legs could carry him, closing the door behind him in an attempt to contain the reek.

Unlike anything he had endured in many years, Hank soon discovered what a challenge descending the stairs was. He winced at the intense back pain surging down his legs with each step and leaned hard on the banister to reduce the stress on his lower body.

By the time he reached the bottom, he felt light-headed, a combined result of his physical anguish and lingering queasiness. He steadied himself against the wall, taking heavy recovery breaths of the unfouled air to slowly regain his composure.

The dining room table caught Hank's attention. He scratched his head while carefully counting the place settings, then recounted them once again. *Four.* He had set a fifth, hadn't he? Yes, without a doubt—he had set it before burying Eliza for the first time. So, where was the fifth place setting?

Hank shook his head slowly and turned away. He waddled into the parlor, lowering himself onto the couch in front of the television with a groan. The machine came to life when he inserted the tape into the VHS player.

As the tape rewound, Hank's mind buzzed with questions of what it would reveal. Who was the evil stranger? Was the perpetrator of this inhuman act even a person? If so, would Hank recognize them, or would the video somehow provide no answers, only deepening the demented mystery? Like some maddening variation of the day prior, when the image revealed little more than a shadowy blob shifting in the nighttime storm.

His stomach churned as he twisted the hankie between his fingers, his chest seizing with the unbearable suspense. Tiny beads of sweat sprang from his forehead, belying the coolness of the house. The recurring thought of a cigarette snuck back into his head yet again, but he gave the craving no heed.

After a torturous wait, the tape ended with a click, fraying Hank's tightly wound nerves.

He pressed PLAY on the remote control and slid forward to anchor himself on the edge of the couch. *And now, the moment of truth...,* he thought, but then he recalled that he had said the same thing the morning prior, yet truth had evaded him.

His own face filled the screen. Hank Mitchell stepped back from the closet, arranged the clothing, and then held up both hands, fingers crossed. "Please don't fail me." The image was sharp, the room well illuminated—a remarkable contrast to the prior night's grainy, distorted video of the graveyard.

The camera blurred and then auto-focused as he crossed the room, adjusting once more when he disappeared from the frame, settling on the open doorway. Several anxious breaths later, the hall lights blinked off, rendering the entry a portal into darkness.

Hank pressed the FAST-FORWARD button, and the machine began to hum. Horizontal bands of video snow rolled from the bottom of the screen to the top, with cycles of thin, white stripes serving as the only indication that the tape was advancing.

Watching intently, Hank licked his dry lips with his dry tongue, then wiped his brow with the handkerchief using both hands while rubbing his temples. Nothing happened on the screen for what seemed like an awful long time.

All at once, the hall illuminated, and a shadow appeared on the corridor's wall. Goose flesh bristled on Hank's arms. With his hands shaking almost uncontrollably, steering his thumb to the PLAY button proved tricky.

A wave of nausea passed over him again. He pressed his palms against his cheeks, trying desperately to counter the swooning feeling. The shadow on the wall shifted as its source proceeded toward the bedroom doorway.

Hank held his breath in heart-wrenching anticipation as the rest of the world fell away. His heart pounded so hard he could actually hear it, beating in perfect rhythm to the throbbing in his temples. A drop of sweat rolled down over his eyebrow and into his eye, and he blinked away the sting without detaching his gape from the television.

The figure turned from the hall and stepped inside the doorway, but the picture blurred as the camera lost its focus. When the auto-focus corrected, the gravedigger resolved into clear view. Hank stared at the video screen—crisp, yet wholly unintelligible. He squinted at first, then his eyes grew wide. Time dilated while he struggled to piece together the dumbfounding image on the tube.

A stabbing sensation stuck Hank in the sternum, shot up his spine into his skull, and rebounded downward, settling as a cramp in his gut. His stomach lurched, and he covered his mouth to stifle the gag. His vision went fuzzy as a flicker of understanding registered in his brain. When the parlor came back into focus, his facial expression resolved into a visage of wretched comprehension, with confusion giving way to despair.

On the television screen the picture wobbled in and out of focus, then settled on Hank Mitchell walking toward the bed carrying a muddy bundle against his chest. Tears streamed down his cheeks as he gingerly laid Eliza's corpse on the bed, unwrapping her from the saturated quilt. Standing over her, he tenderly wiped the dirt from her gruesome face, combing her stringy hair with his fingers. He reached out and touched the silver broach, rubbing it slowly with his thumb.

"I'm so sorry, dear," Hank whispered between sobs on the TV screen, "I never should've done it." He leaned over and kissed the puffy, greenish-gray forehead of the Eliza-corpse, spilling teardrops from each eye onto her swollen cheek. Consumed with heartache, he lingered beside his wife for a minute, then stepped back from the bed, turned, and left the room.

The video returned to the static image of the bedroom, almost identical to the earlier scene, except with the addition of Eliza Mitchell's rotting body on the bed, frozen in lifelessness.

⚬

Hank released his trapped lungful of air, replacing it with an unsteady rhythm of shallow wheezes. Too beleaguered to even think, he remained motionless on the couch as the minutes ticked away, stacking in sequence until an hour had passed, then another. He lingered in a catatonic state while morning lapsed into afternoon.

Eventually, he sniffed and wiped his eyes and nose with his hankie. He rubbed his aching temples, throbbing from the lack of caffeine. After tucking the handkerchief into his pocket, he pushed up from the couch, staggered across the room, and pulled open the front door.

On the front veranda, the cold air seeped through Hank's robe almost instantly, but he felt numb to it. He stepped up to the railing while he stared into the distance, taking in the sight of Ghoul

House, now clearly visible through the mostly bare trees. Nothing but an old, abandoned house, steadily sinking into nature. A benign remnant of the past, gradually slipping toward oblivion.

Hank wiped his face with both hands, turned away, and plodded toward his front door, which he'd left cocked ajar. The warmth of the house barely registered as he inched back into the parlor.

Hank halted in his tracks beside the dining room table, nodding at the sight of four place settings, understanding now what had happened to the fifth. He wandered over to the cabinet and removed matching dishes and utensils, arranging them on the table so each of the six seats had a place setting.

He moved on to the kitchen, where he measured out two tablespoons of grounds from the Folgers can, filled the reservoir halfway to the mineral line, and switched on the coffeemaker.

As the appliance gurgled, he wandered to the back door and looked out at the cemetery, squinting at the dirt piled beside Eliza's grave, holding his glare until the coffeemaker belched its final puff of steam.

Hank pulled the John Deere mug out of the strainer, filled it with coffee, and lifted it to his lips. A big swallow scorched his mouth and throat, but he savored the pain and took another.

After putting the mug down, he reached behind the sugar canister to fish out the vial of Xylazine. He removed the rubber stopper and tipped the tiny bottle over the coffee, dumping the entire contents in, then stirred the potion with a teaspoon. Three gulps later, he carried the cup to the stairs and began climbing, using the banister to hoist his spent body up each step.

Hank held the coffee mug to his mouth, breathing in the steam and taking small sips while he shuffled on baby steps down the hall and into Eliza's bedroom. He crossed the room, circling beyond the mess of vomit, and stalled before Brenda's desk. A warm, woozy sensation filled his head as he looked over the framed photo of mother and daughter, the ribbons on the wall, the books, and the lava lamp that had not been illuminated since 1972. After another swig of coffee, he peeked into the cup. Half gone.

Feeling no more pain, Hank took several sideways steps and propped himself against the edge of the bed. No longer sensing any foul odor, he lifted the mug to his mouth and took several more gulps to finish it. He bent over, placed the empty cup on the floor, dropped to his side, and rolled onto his back.

Pulsating veins of color shimmered on the ceiling. After stretching out beside Eliza, he turned to look her way. She no longer looked so gruesome. "Hi dear," he said, sliding his hand over to take hold of hers.

The faint sound of horses and buggies arose, peaked, and then gradually trailed off into silence.

A warm vibration rumbled through Hank's body, and his ears filled with white noise. As he grew heavier, he sank further into the bed. His eyelids rolled closed, the vibrant colors dulled, and the peaceful thrum softened as his senses blended together.

A heavenly calm overcame Hank Mitchell as his world dimmed into utter blackness.

EPILOGUE

SPRING

DARKNESS, WEIGHTLESSNESS, AND ABSOLUTE stillness enveloped Hank, as though he were floating in the cosmos. Timelessness infused whatever sense of awareness he retained as he drifted into nothingness.

By and by, from the periphery of the void, a glow began to emerge, like the frost on a window, beginning as a border, gradually spreading inward until it filled the entire pane. Hank watched as it bloomed into a rich plum color, then lightened, shifting into violet. The purple brushed up against his soul, then pressed inside. He relaxed and let it overtake him. Wafting in this vast sea of purple, hearing and feeling nothing, Hank lost all sense of time and place.

As quick as a lightning bolt, the purple cleared in a glaring white flash, and silence lifted, revealing the sound of chirping birds.

Birds?

Like springtime, Hank thought, working to peel open his eyes. Light filled the room. Sunlight, along with a strange lavender glow on one side of his blurry peripheral vision.

Hank detected the scent of ozone, like the smell his power drill caused.

Unable to move anything but his eyelids, he blinked and strained to focus. A while later, he managed to turn his head, rolling steadily toward the lavender color.

The lava lamp. Illuminated.

Within, a pink blob twisted and tumbled, casting swirling shadows on the wall.

Hank rolled his head the opposite way...toward Eliza. Except her side of the mattress was empty. Eliza's favorite quilt—the pink quilt she'd sown for Brenda when she was young—covered the bed, more vibrant than he remembered, and perfectly clean.

One of Hank's fingers twitched. He tried to move it again, and, with considerable effort, eventually succeeded. One by one, he worked on unfreezing his others, and before long, was able to splay out his fingers on both hands and rotate his wrists.

Next came his arms, which, after a while, he regained full movement of, followed by his legs. When he could bend his knees, raising them toward the ceiling, he shifted his focus to his torso.

Once he regained the movement of his full body, Hank pulled himself upright. He swung his legs down to the floor and shifted onto his feet. It took him a moment to reestablish his balance, but he marveled at how he felt no pain whatsoever.

He took a step, then another, ambling over to the open window. A pleasant, warm breeze blew, billowing the curtains inward against him, tickling his face.

The grass held the color of emerald green, and the trees flushed with newly budded leaves, flowers blossoming on the buckeye tree. Birds flew by while others warbled and trilled.

Springtime.

Hank studied the buckeye tree while rubbing his chin. There was something different about it. Then it hit him: the tree, which had been a sapling he and Jimmy had transplanted when they were boys, didn't completely block his view of the barn. It was *smaller*—like half the size he was used to seeing.

Hank withdrew from the window and headed into the hall, following it to the stairway. When he reached the bottom, he looked around the parlor. The furniture was arranged differently. The daybed had no bedsheets or blankets, and Eliza's wheelchair, which he had tucked into the corner, was nowhere in sight.

He wandered to the back of the house, passing the dining room, the table configured with only three place settings.

In the kitchen, he stopped at the open doorway, studying the outside scene through the screen door. The old roofed wooden well structure was back—Eliza's cherished wishing well—the one he had removed when it became rotted beyond repair and replaced with the old grindstone well cap.

Hank retrieved his hat from the hook behind the door. He turned it over in his hands, recognizing it as his mangy hat...except it was too clean, too bright, too stiff. Wedging it onto his head, he pushed open the screen door and stepped out onto the stoop.

"Dad!"

The voice, which seemed to come from inside his head, sounded familiar, but he couldn't immediately place it in his groggy state.

"Mom! Look! It's Dad!"

Hank turned to see Brenda, standing in the vegetable garden, wearing the "Sweet Pea" shirt, pointing his way. Eliza, kneeling near her daughter, appearing as she had in her forties, pulled her bonnet from her head and wiped the sweat from her face with the back of her sleeve. With clear eyes, she turned her gaze in the direction Brenda was pointing and grinned.

Hank leaped off into the grass, bolting toward his wife and daughter, running faster than he had moved in decades. He had missed them so much, but winter had passed. It was springtime now, and the family was together once again.

AFTERWORD

WHEN I WAS TWELVE years old, I heard about this very intriguing made-for-television movie that was soon going to air: *Sybil*, about a young woman who developed "split personalities." I wanted to see this program so badly, but alas, my mother didn't deem it appropriate, so I missed out.

The idea of this condition, technically known as "dissociative identity disorder," fascinated and terrified me. I don't know much about psychology, and although decades have passed, I still have never seen *Sybil*. But in my uninformed mind, I imagined trauma could lead to split personalities as a coping means.

Somewhere along the line, I got to thinking about the concept of having to make a decision that is so difficult, that the human psyche can't deal with the internal conflict, causing it to split into two parts: half deciding one way, the other half deciding the opposite.

You may recognize this as the demise of our poor friend Hank Mitchell, whose nighttime personality made a futile attempt to undo a deed he couldn't go along with. And so, in a way, Mercy Killing is: Sybil meets Georg Carl Tanzler (also known as Count Carl von Cosel). While the former qualifies as a household name, there's a good chance you haven't heard of the latter. I promise you it's worth looking him up.

As I worked through the final rounds of revisions on this book, my beloved father came down with pneumonia. It was gut-wrenching to watch him struggle with the illness and its complications, taking such a sudden turn from being a healthy and active man, despite being nearly 94 years old. Sadly, his condition worsened, and we moved him into hospice care before he passed away. I had been given a real-life dose of some of the themes I had explored in Hank and Eliza Mitchell's world. When I got back on my feet and reengaged in writing, I found myself wondering if I would see the need to revise anything in their story. As it turned out, I didn't change much. I did, however, know who to dedicate the book to.

I understand how sensitive the themes of this story are and I consciously tried to avoid taking a moral position, other than allowing Hank to consider his circumstances and decide for himself how to act. His fateful decisions provided the foundation for his dark journey, but perhaps the turn of events that followed might serve as a cautionary tale. Alas, there are no simple answers when it comes to these matters.

Clarkton and Homer County, Ohio are fictional renderings but are fashioned in my imagination from areas of Coshocton, Holmes, and Tuscarawas Counties I regularly venture to. The inspiration for Shirley Gould's farmhouse is an old, derelict home hidden away on my cousin's property in Coshocton County. I'd guess it's been abandoned for over 100 years, although buzzards have been nesting in it since I was a kid.

I feel drawn to this beautiful region in the Ohio countryside, although I also wonder: am I alone in feeling it conceals a lonesome and haunting presence?

ACKNOWLEDGEMENTS

AS CRAZY AS IT sounds, *Mercy Killing* was at least 35 years in the making. I first wrote the story in the 1980s, saving it on an ancient floppy drive that I subsequently lost. I wrote it again in the early 2000s but never attempted to publish it. As I learned more about the writing craft, I realized the manuscript still needed work, but I didn't know how to fix it. So, when I got serious about writing a few years ago, I put my energy into a brand-new story *(Phantom Realm),* rather than *Mercy Killing.* Once I got *Phantom Realm* out of the way, I found I had some fresh ideas for *Mercy Killing.* After all these years, it's been quite a joyride weaving new elements into the story.

Because I've written, rewritten, and revised this story many times, over many years, many people have helped me along the way, most of whom I've probably forgotten by now. While I won't attempt to acknowledge all those individuals here, I am grateful they encouraged me to stick with it.

I would like to thank my sister-in-law, Dr. Victoria Bowden, who provided medical expertise assistance before I started my rewrite. Then, as the manuscript neared its final state, she served as a beta reader. If the story is medically sound, I have her to thank.

I appreciate the feedback and encouragement from my wife Mary and daughter Kerry, both of whom beta-read an early draft (as well as previous, rougher drafts). Their input helped guide me through some significant structural changes, and their encouragement was invaluable for keeping me plugging away. Thanks to Mary for her never-ending support as I toiled away for untold hours on this story.

The Horror Writers Association assigned Billy Halpin as my mentor while I was working on Phantom Realm. I appreciate the HWA for this, and I appreciate Billy for continuing to help me, including beta-reading this story. When he came back with an extensive write-up of comments and suggestions, I stifled a groan, because it looked like a lot of work. But his feedback was excellent, so I went back to it.

I workshopped some of the rewritten chapters of this book with some of my horror writing colleagues, with whom I've been participating in monthly critique sessions over the past couple of years. Through that process, Kelly Griffiths, Sean Seebach, Rami Ungar, Ann Heyward, and Randall Drum helped me shape the story into what it is. I have learned so much through our workshops, and I cherish our camaraderie.

Speaking of Kelly Griffiths and Sean Seebach, both have become trusted critique partners, and each helped me improve the full *Mercy Killing* manuscript through their editorial reviews.

Speaking one more time of Kelly, she was the model on the book cover. Before you flip back to look at the cover, I can assure you, Kelly doesn't look like that digitally enhanced character! When I asked Kelly if she'd be willing to climb into a muddy hole in the woods at night, I expected either a "no way!" or a reluctant "okay." What I got instead was something more like "hell, yes!"

I'm grateful to my brother-in-law Chris Esch, who prepared and shot the cover photo of Kelly, and then added digital artistic flourishes. All this took more time than you would expect, and Chris is great at thinking everything through. I should also mention that Chris produced my author photo as well, so I'm extra appreciative of him for that.

I'd like to thank DM Guay for sharing her knowledge and experience in book marketing. I know I need to be doing much more of that book marketing stuff. But for now, the fun part for me of being an author is the writing. Maybe someday I'll get there, and in the meantime, I *am* listening to everything she says.

Finally, I'd like to thank *you* for reading. Knowing someone has read something I wrote makes all the hours I toiled on it worthwhile. I'd especially like to acknowledge those readers who read my debut novel and decided they liked it enough that they'd read my next book when it was eventually published, which motivated me to get it done. Either way, I hope you liked *Mercy Killing.* I can only hope you'll be looking forward to reading *Atrocity,* which I'll be working on next.

ABOUT THE AUTHOR

A FANATIC OF ALL things dark and creepy, Neil Sater lives with his wife, Mary, in the Cleveland, Ohio area. They have two grown children and two grandchildren. Having spent his career doing other things, Neil is happy to be now finding time for writing. His debut novel, *Phantom Realm: The Haunting of Misery Mansion*, earned the #1 New Release rating in Young Adult Ghost Stories. A member of the Horror Writers Association, he's currently working on *Atrocity*, a horror novel also based in Homer County, Ohio.

Sign up for Neil Sater's newsletter through his website:

https://authorsater.com/

Printed in Great Britain
by Amazon

49810611R00138